PUFFIN BOOKS

Fifteen

Beverly Cleary was born in Oregon, USA, and lived in a town so small it had no library until her mother arranged to have books sent and acted as librarian in a room over a bank, and there Beverly Cleary learned to love books. She spent much of her childhood either with books or on her way to and from the library. After graduating from the University of California at Berkeley, she went to the School of Librarianship in Seattle, Washington, and specialized in library work with children. She was Children's Librarian in Yakima, Washington and an Army Librarian in Oakland, California during World War II. Beverly Cleary is the mother of twins, now grown up, and lives in California. She has won many awards for her books, which have been translated into many languages.

Other books by Beverly Cleary

Young Puffin

HERE COME THE TWINS

In Puffin

HENRY AND BEEZUS
BEEZUS AND RAMONA
RAMONA AND HER FATHER
RAMONA AND HER MOTHER
RAMONA QUIMBY, AGE 8
RAMONA THE BRAVE
RAMONA THE PEST
RAMONA FOREVER

DEAR MR HENSHAW
THE MOUSE AND THE MOTORCYCLE
RALPH S. MOUSE
STRIDER

BEVERLY CLEARY

Fifteen

PUFFIN BOOKS

PUFFIN BOOKS

Published by the Penguin Group
Penguin Books Ltd, 27 Wrights Lane, London W8 5TZ, England
Penguin Books USA Inc., 375 Hudson Street, New York, New York 10014, USA
Penguin Books Australia Ltd, Ringwood, Victoria, Australia
Penguin Books Canada Ltd, 10 Alcorn Avenue, Toronto, Ontario, Canada M4V 3B2
Penguin Books (NZ) Ltd, 182–190 Wairau Road, Auckland 10, New Zealand

Penguin Books Ltd, Registered Offices: Harmondsworth, Middlesex, England

First published in the USA 1956
First published in Great Britain in Peacock Books 1962
Reissued in Puffin Books 1977
Reprinted in Penguin Books 1988
Reissued in Puffin Books 1995
5 7 9 10 8 6 4

Printed in England by Clays Ltd, St Ives plc
Set in Monotype Baskerville

CHAPTER

I

TODAY I'm going to meet a boy, Jane Purdy told herself, as she walked up Blossom Street toward her baby-sitting job. *Today I'm going to meet a boy*. If she thought it often enough as if she really believed it, maybe she actually would meet a boy even though she was headed for Sandra Norton's house and the worst baby-sitting job in Woodmont.

If I don't step on any cracks in the sidewalk all the way there, Jane thought, I'll be sure to meet a boy. But avoiding cracks was silly, of course, and the sort of thing she had done when she was in the third grade. She was being just as silly as some of the other fifteen-year-old girls she knew, who counted red convertibles and believed they would go steady with the first boy they saw after the hundredth red convertible. Counting convertibles and not stepping on cracks were no way to meet a boy.

Maybe, when she finished her job with Sandra, she could walk down to Nibley's Confectionery and Soda Fountain and sit at the counter and order a chocolate soda, and if she sipped it very, very slowly a new boy might happen to come in and sit down beside her. He would be old enough to have a driver's licence, and he would have crinkles around his eyes that showed he had a sense of humour and he would be tall, the kind of boy all the other girls would like to date. Their eyes would meet in the mirror behind the milk shake machines, and he would

5

smile and she would smile back and he would turn to her and look down (*down* – that was important) and grin and say . . .

'Hello there!' A girl's voice interrupted Jane's daydream, and she looked up to see Marcy Stokes waving at her from a green convertible driven by Greg Donahoe, president of the junior class of Woodmont High School.

'Hi, Marcy,' Jane called back. People who said, 'Hello there', to her always made her feel so unimportant.

Greg waved, and as the couple drove on down the hill Marcy brushed a lock of hair out of her eyes and smiled back at Jane with the kind of smile a girl riding in a convertible with a popular boy on a summer day gives a girl who is walking alone. And that smile made Jane feel that everything about herself was all wrong. Her yellow cotton dress was too – well too little-girlish with its round collar and full skirt. Her skin wasn't tan enough and, even if it were, she didn't have a white piqué dress to show it off. And her curly brown hair, which had seemed pretty enough in the mirror at home, now seemed childish compared to Marcy's sleek blonde hair, bleached to golden streaks by the sun.

The trouble with me, Jane thought, as the hill grew steeper, is that I am not the cashmere-sweater type like Marcy. Marcy wore her cashmere sweaters as if they were of no importance at all. Jane had one cashmere sweater, which she took off the minute she got home from school. Marcy had many dates with the most popular boys in school and spent a lot of time with the crowd at Nibley's. Jane had an occasional date with an old family friend named George, who was an inch shorter than she was and carried his money in a change purse instead of loose in his pocket and took her straight home from the movies. Marcy had her name mentioned in the gossip column of the *Woodmontonian* nearly every week. Jane had her name in the school paper when she served on entertainment committees. Marcy belonged. Jane did not.

And if I were in Marcy's place right now, Jane thought wistfully, I wouldn't even know what to say. I would probably just sit there beside Greg with my hands all clammy, because I would be so nervous and excited.

Jane reached the end of Blossom Street and paused to catch her breath before starting to climb the winding road to Sandra's house. She looked back through the locust trees at the roof of her own comfortable old house in the centre of Woodmont. In recent years this pleasant village had begun to grow in two directions. Toward the bay, on the treeless side of town, there was now a housing development called Bayaire Estates – block after block of small houses, all variations of one style, which Jane thought of as the no-down-payment section, because of the advertisements on the boards along the highway. On the other side of Purdys' part of town, where Woodmont rose sharply into tree-covered hills, there were also many new houses, referred to in advertisements as 'California modern, architect-designed, planned for outdoor living'. These houses were being built into the hillside among the gracious old redwood homes, now called 'charming rustics'.

It was toward one of these new houses in the hills that Jane now walked so reluctantly. Eight-year-old Sandra Norton and her parents had lived in Woodmont only a few months, having recently returned after two years in France, where Mr Norton had been the American representative of an airline. Already Sandra was notorious among Woodmont baby-sitters. The last time Jane sat with her, Sandra had grabbed a Flit gun full of fly spray and aimed it at a new chair upholstered in pale fabric. Before Jane wrested the Flit gun from Sandra she was drenched in fly spray. Afterwards she had laughed about the incident and turned it into a funny paragraph for a baby-sitting (baby-running was really a better word) article she had written for Manuscript, the Woodmont High literary club. Nevertheless, it was not an experience she would care to repeat.

When Jane reached the Norton house, which was set on a flat area bulldozed out of the side of the hill, she found Sandra, dressed in a cow-girl costume, in the front yard bending over a bed of snapdragons. Her blonde hair, with its uncared-for permanent wave, hung like ravelled rope on either side of her thin little face.

Jane walked across the tender new lawn. 'Hello, Sandra,' she said cheerfully. 'What are you doing?'

'Catching flies and shutting them up inside snap-dragons,' replied Sandra, without looking at Jane. An angry buzzing came from the blossoms in front of her.

Jane noticed Sandra's mother looking impatiently through the picture window so she hurried to the front door, which Mrs Norton opened at once. She was wearing a silk suit the colour of sand and a tiny pink hat smothered in flowers and misted with veiling. Jane felt young and dowdy beside her.

'Hello there, Jane,' said Mrs Norton breathlessly. 'I was so afraid I couldn't get anyone to look after Sandra, and I didn't want to miss the hospital guild's tea and fashion show. See that she rests, won't you? She went to the city with us last night and she's a little bit tired today.'

'Yes, Mrs Norton,' answered Jane. That made two people in a row who had said, 'Hello there'.

Mrs Norton swept past Jane, leaving a cloud of expensive scent (probably Chanel Number Five, Jane decided, since Sandra's mother had been living in France), and then she paused. 'Oh, yes – and don't let Cuthbert out of the house. We just had him shampooed and I don't want him rolling in the dirt. It takes weeks to get an appointment to have a dog washed. It's worse than trying to get an appointment at the hairdresser's.' Her high heels clicked down the brick walk. 'Goodbye, chick,' she called to Sandra.

'I want you to stay home.' Sandra stared unhappily at her mother.

'I'll be back before you know it,' Mrs Norton said with artificial gaiety, and hopped into her car.

Jane was alone with Sandra. She walked across the grass to join the child, who was still occupied with the buzzing snapdragons. 'Come on, Sandra,' she said. 'I'll help you let the flies out of the flowers before we go into the house for your rest.'

Sandra, who was holding a fly by the wings, pinched open the mouth of a blossom and popped the fly inside. 'My mother said I didn't have to rest,' she told Jane.

Now what do I do, Jane wondered. That was the trouble with baby-sitting. Mothers always told sitters what to do with their children, but they rarely told them how to do it. Perhaps if she did not mention the rest she could entice Sandra into the house and read to her until she fell asleep. 'If you were a fly, would you like to be shut up in a snapdragon?' Jane asked, to change the subject.

9

'No. That's why I'm doing it,' said Sandra. 'My mother said Julie was going to sit with me.'

'Julie couldn't come, because she had to sit with Jackie,' Jane explained. Julie was her best friend. The two girls often handed over baby-sitting jobs to each other. The only reason Jane was sitting with Sandra today was that she and Julie felt that some day they might be broke enough to really need to sit with Sandra and so in the meantime it would be a good idea to keep Mrs Norton's business.

'I'd rather have Julie than you,' said Sandra flatly.

Maybe she would, thought Jane. Julie was such a comfortable, cheerful person that all the children liked her. But this was not getting Sandra into the house and persuading her to go to sleep. And if she could not do that, Jane knew that she was in for a long and difficult afternoon. 'I know what,' she said brightly, as if she had just had an idea.

Sandra looked at her suspiciously. She was, Jane knew, a child who had had many baby-sitters and was undoubtedly on to all the tricks of getting her to be obedient.

'Let's go in the house and see what Cuthbert is doing.' Jane held out her hand to Sandra. Into the house – that was the first step toward a nap.

'He's asleep under the coffee table,' said Sandra. 'That's all he ever does. He's a dumb dog. I'd rather have a horse.' Sandra stared at Jane as if she were taking her measure to see just how far she could go with this sitter.

Why is it, Jane wondered, that substitute teachers and baby-sitters are so often targets for children?

'O.K., let's go in the house,' agreed Sandra suddenly.

Jane could not help wondering uneasily what the glint in Sandra's eye meant. She hoped she could figure out a way to get Sandra to sleep quickly, because there were so many things indoors that she could get into mischief with – knick-knacks that could be broken, lamps to be knocked over, lipstick for marking wallpaper. After the experience with the Flit gun Jane knew she could not trust Sandra for one instant.

Jane glanced around the Nortons' living-room, so different from her own home, where everything was comfortably worn. 'A house is meant to be lived in,' her mother often said. Here everything looked brand-new, as if the furniture had been delivered only the day before. The wooden pieces were square and simple and, except for a few cushions in brilliant colours, everything in the room was carefully neutral. Over the fireplace hung a painting made up of drips and dribbles, splotches and splashes, in the same colours as the cushions. The room looked, Jane decided, interior-decorated. Not even the layer of dust or the heap of magazines and newspapers on the coffee table or the overflowing ash trays made the room seem as if a family really lived here. And isn't it funny, Jane thought; if I were blindfolded and set down in the house of any one of my baby-sitting customers I could tell where I was by the odour of the house. The Nortons' house smelled of fresh plaster and wallpaper and stale cigarette smoke.

Cuthbert was, as Sandra had predicted, asleep under the coffee table. Now the fat pug dog rose and shook himself, scattering his hair over the carpet. He was an ugly little animal with a black face on a tan body, popeyes, and a nose so upturned that it was difficult for him to breathe. Panting asthmatically, he ran toward Jane, his kinky tail wagging, his bulging eyes beseeching her for attention. She knelt and patted his head. Cuthbert was overcome with emotion; his breathing rasped louder, and he ran back and forth under the edge of the coffee table to scratch his back. Then he collapsed on the rug and panted.

Sandra opened the front door. 'I'm going to let Cuthbert out,' she cried. 'Here, Cuthbert!'

'Oh, no, Sandra,' protested Jane. 'Your mother said not to. He's just been washed.'

But Cuthbert was not going to miss this rare opportunity for freedom. As fast as his short little legs would carry him, he scrambled out of the front door and down the steps.

'Oh, Sandra,' said Jane reproachfully, and ran after the dog, who had scurried down the brick walk and across the lawn.

'Go, on, Cuthbert!' shrieked Sandra, jumping up and down in the doorway. Cuthbert scuttled under a bush.

Don't roll in the dirt, Jane pleaded silently. Please don't roll in the dirt when you've just been washed. She got down on her hands and knees and crawled under the bush toward the dog, who puffed and wheezed as he watched her with his bulging eyes.

'Don't let her get you, Cuthbert,' screamed Sandra.

A branch caught in Jane's hair and while she worked to disentangle it, Cuthbert stopped wheezing and began to bark. A car horn tooted on the road.

Oh! though Jane, as she looked toward the kerb. Oh no! Greg and Marcy, headed up the hill in the green convertible, were looking at her and laughing.

'Hi,' Jane called, trying to sound gay.

'Why don't you bark back at him?' Marcy asked, and Greg laughed and drove on.

Jane felt her face grow hot with embarrassment. Greg's laugh she did not mind, because it was a friendly laugh; but she did not like to be laughed at by a girl riding in a convertible. She wished she had come back with an answer, something like, 'I only bark in English and this dog has been living in France.' Jane sighed. That was the trouble with her. She always thought of the right answer too late, or if she did think of it at the right time she was too shy to say it.

Jane dived farther under the bush and caught Cuthbert by one foreleg. He yapped hoarsely and hysterically while she dragged him out and picked him up. He wheezed and snuffled as he tried to wriggle out of her grasp, but she held him tight. Then his chunky little body relaxed and he struggled to get enough air through his turned-up nose. Poor thing, thought Jane; I believe he's relieved to be caught. He wouldn't know what to do with his freedom if he had it.

She hurried up the brick walk with the fat little dog in her arms. And this was the day I was sure I would meet a boy, she thought. And now look at me – all rumpled, with leaves in my hair and grass stains on my skirt. Jane noticed apprehensively that Sandra was no longer in the doorway. Certainly the child would not be sleepy after the excitement of making her sitter chase Cuthbert. But she found Sandra sitting quietly in a chair looking at a copy of *Vogue*. Jane carefully shut the door and shoved Cuthbert under the coffee table.

'Hello,' said Sandra, as if she were surprised to see Jane so soon. Cuthbert began to snore.

'Hello.' Jane eyed her charge. Sandra's thin little face did look tired – so tired that Jane felt sorry for her. Since she was willing to sit quietly looking at *Vogue*, perhaps she was one step closer to a nap. 'Why don't we go to your room?' Jane suggested gently. 'I'll read to you.'

When Sandra ignored her and went on reading *Vogue*, Jane sat down. To have Sandra fall asleep over *Vogue* was too much to hope for, she knew, but she did not know what to do next. Sandra put her feet on the coffee table.

'Oh, Sandra, I wouldn't put my feet on the table if I were you,' said Jane.

Sandra stared at her over the top of the magazine. 'Say table in French,' she demanded.

'*La table*,' answered Jane, giving the article as well as the noun, as she had been taught to do in her one year of high-school French. Well, she thought hopefully, maybe we can work out a nice quiet game with French. I'll say something in French and then Sandra can say something in French. Maybe that will amuse her.

'Say chair,' ordered Sandra.

'*La chaise*,' answered Jane promptly. Those A's she had earned in two semesters of French were going to come in handy after all.

'Window,' Sandra said.

'*La fenêtre*.' That was easy. Practically the first word Jane had learned in French.

'Curtains,' demanded Sandra.

Jane paused. Curtains? Oh, yes. '*Les rideaux*.'

Sandra looked impressed and Jane relaxed. This could go on for a long time, and as long as Sandra asked the French for ordinary objects in the living-room she was confident that she could answer.

'Dog.' Cuthbert's snoring called Sandra's attention to the dog.

'*Le chien.*'

'Book.'

'*Le livre.*'

Sandra put down *Vogue* and began to wander around the room looking for new objects to name. 'Desk,' she said.

Jane started to say *le pupitre* but remembered that was the word for a pupil's desk. '*Le bureau*,' she answered, pleased with herself for remembering the difference. However, she had begun to notice that the room was full of objects that her French vocabulary was not equal to. 'Now you tell me the word for rug,' she suggested, because she herself did not know the word and did not want to risk revealing her ignorance to Sandra.

'*Le tapis*,' answered Sandra promptly and in an accent more authentic than Jane's.

'*C'est bien!*' cried Jane, feeling that she sounded like her own French teacher, even though she had no idea whether Sandra was right or not.

'You speak French sort of funny,' observed Sandra critically, as her eyes darted around the room looking for a difficult object to name. Her eye fell on a heavy crystal ash tray on the desk. 'Ash tray,' she said.

Ash tray? Tray of the ashes? It was not the sort of phrase one learned in first-year French. Jane gave up. 'I'm sorry, Sandra, I don't know how to say ash tray in French.'

Sandra picked up the overflowing crystal tray. 'Say it, or I'll dump it on the rug!'

Jane began to feel uneasy. Maybe she could make up something, some syllables that sounded foreign. No, Sandra would know the difference. 'I'm sorry, Sandra,' she said. 'I just don't know it. Put down the ash tray and let's try something else.'

Sandra looked defiantly at Jane. Slowly she tipped the ash tray so that ashes and lipstick-stained cigarette butts cascaded on to the beige carpet.

'Sandra!' cried Jane.

Sandra set the ash tray back on the desk and snatched a bottle of ink out of a drawer. 'Say bottle of blue ink,' she ordered, as she loosened the top of the bottle. 'Say it or I'll dump it on the rug!'

That's one I know, Jane told herself, but the words would not come to her lips. She could read *Permanent Blue Black* on the label of the ink bottle. She looked in despair at the ashes and cigarette butts on the pale carpet – wall-to-wall carpet, yards and yards of it. The permanent blue-black ink would fall in a permanent blue-black puddle and seep slowly ... If she made a grab for Sandra and tried to get the bottle away from her, the ink was sure to spill in the scuffle.

'Say it!' Sandra sounded ominous.

'Uh ... le ... la,' was all that Jane could utter. Oh, why couldn't she think! Bottle? Bottle? What *was* the word for bottle? 'Wait a minute,' she pleaded desperately. 'It's on the tip of my tongue.' It was, but she could not find it. And Sandra, she knew from her experience with the fly spray, was ruthless.

'You don't know it.' There was triumph in Sandra's voice. 'I know something you don't know! I know something you don't know!'

Jane was desperate. She could not think and she was afraid to move. Those yards and yards of beige carpet ... It would be ruined and she would be responsible. Yards and yards of carpet covered with permanent blue-black stains . . .

At that moment Jane heard the back door open. 'Good afternoon, Mrs Norton,' a boy's cheerful voice called. Cuthbert scrambled out from under the coffee table and ran yapping joyfully into the kitchen.

Startled that someone should burst into the house without knocking, Jane still was unable to move. She could only think, The ink, Sandra, the ink. Don't spill the ink. *Please* don't spill the permanent blue-black ink.

There was the sound of the refrigerator door opening and closing and a voice saying, 'Hi there, Cuthbert. How's the fellow?'

Jane knew she should investigate, but she could not leave Sandra with the ink bottle in her hands. 'Who is it?' she called out in a weak voice.

'The Doggie Diner,' the strange voice answered, and a boy appeared in the dining-room doorway. 'Oh, excuse me. I thought you were Mrs Norton,' he said.

If only this intrusion would distract Sandra from the ink! 'The Doggie Diner?' Jane echoed, and then felt stupid for doing so. She knew that the Doggie Diner was a small business that delivered horse meat to the owners of dogs in Woodmont and nearby towns. It was just that she was so startled to have a boy appear from nowhere. And, now that she took her eyes away from the ink bottle long enough to look at him, a very nice strange boy.

'I brought Cuthbert's meat. Mrs Norton likes me to walk in and put it in the refrigerator for her,' he explained, looking questioningly at Jane.

'Oh. I'm – I'm sitting with Sandra.' Jane felt that the way he looked at her required an answer.

'Yes, and she can't say bottle of blue ink in French, so I'm going to dump this on the rug,' said Sandra.

'Oh, Sandra,' pleaded Jane wearily, 'please put the ink down.'

Sandra tipped the bottle at a dangerous angle. Now that she had an audience she was going to make the most of her scene. 'Say it,' she ordered. 'Say it right now.'

'*Utpay atthay ownday!*' commanded the strange boy in a sharp voice.

Sandra turned from Jane to stare at him. 'What did you say?' she wanted to know.

Utpay atthay ownday? Utpay – of course! Suddenly Jane laughed. The boy was saying, 'Put that down,' in pig Latin and he had succeeded in diverting Sandra. '*Esyay, Andrasay, utpay atthay ownday,*' she said, and smiled gratefully at him over Sandra's head.

Sandra turned to Jane. 'What are you saying? I can't understand you.' She looked close to tears.

'I was telling you to put the ink down,' answered Jane.

Sandra was intrigued by this language she could not understand. 'Say some more. You've got to say some more.'

'You didn't put the ink down,' Jane pointed out, and looked at the strange boy again.

'Yes, put it down,' he said, and Jane felt a ripple of pleasure that this boy was standing by her when she needed him. Reluctantly Sandra walked over to the desk and set the ink down. Jane and the strange boy exchanged looks – relief and gratitude on her part, amusement on his.

'Well, so long,' said the boy, and disappeared from the dining-room doorway.

I mustn't let him get away like this, thought Jane, and ran to the kitchen just as he was going out the back door. 'Thanks a lot,' she called out to him. 'I don't know what I would have done if you hadn't come along.'

'That's O.K.,' he said. 'I've got a kid sister and I know how it is.' And with that he was gone.

Jane looked out the kitchen window in time to see him jump into a red truck with *Doggie Diner – Fresh U.S. Government-inspected Horse Meat Delivered Weekly* painted on its side. And in a moment the truck was disappearing around a bend in the road.

Well, thought Jane. Well! I did meet a boy today! A new boy who is old enough to have a driver's licence!

'Say some more,' demanded Sandra, bringing Jane's thoughts back into the kitchen.

'Come to your room and I'll say some more.' Jane spoke gently, but she had made up her mind to be firm with Sandra from now on. She had the upper hand and she was going to hang on to it as long as she could. 'Come along.'

Somewhat reluctantly, Sandra followed Jane to her room and sat down on the bed, which was covered by a spread woven with a design of cattle brands. The influence of the interior decorator had not reached Sandra's room. Her walls were hung with pictures of blue rabbits and pink kittens that would glow in the dark, and beside her bed was a child-sized papiermâché figure of Bugs Bunny with a real radio set in the middle of its stomach. 'Say some more,' pleaded Sandra.

'*Imetay orfay ouryay apnay.*' Jane took advantage of Sandra's interest to kneel and remove the child's shoes.

'What did you say?' Sandra asked.

'I said it's time for your nap.'

Sandra scowled and looked as if she were about to say it was not time for her nap. Instead she said, 'Is it a foreign language?'

Jane smiled. 'Not exactly. It's more like a secret language.'

'A secret language?' Sandra asked eagerly. 'Do you really know how to talk a secret language?'

'Yes,' replied Jane, thinking how tired Sandra looked. She unfolded the blanket at the foot of the bed. 'Lie down and let me cover you up and I'll say some more things in the secret language.'

Wearily, Sandra flopped back with her head on the pillow. 'Say my name,' she requested, as Jane pulled the blanket over her.

'*Andrasay Ortonnay*,' Jane told her.

'That's pretty,' was Sandra's comment. 'Say your name.'

'*Anejay Urdypay*.' Was Sandra really beginning to look drowsy? Jane watched the little girl's eyelids begin to droop. '*Ogay otay eepslay*,' she said softly.

Sandra's eyes closed and then opened again as she struggled against sleep.

'Sandra,' whispered Jane, 'what is the name of the boy who brought Cuthbert's meat?'

'I don't know,' said Sandra drowsily, and closed her eyes.

Jane sat watching her for a moment. Poor kid, she wasn't really a monster. She was just a tired little girl who had lived in too many places and had too many strange baby-sitters. Jane tucked the blanket over Sandra's arms.

Well, she thought, I'm certainly bright. She had wanted to meet a new boy and when she finally did meet one she didn't even find out his name. All she knew about him was that he delivered horse meat and had a younger sister.

Jane sat staring at the Bugs Bunny with the radio in its stomach, but she did not really see it. Instead, she saw the boy standing in the doorway grinning at her. And when I did meet him, her thoughts ran on, I was rumpled and covered with dirt and grass stains and worried about the Nortons' rug. That was no way to make an impression on a boy. Then she smiled to herself. If any of the boys she already knew delivered horse meat for the Doggie Diner, she would think it was a big joke. Maybe it was funny, but somehow she did not feel like laughing at this boy's job.

Why, I know lots of things about him, Jane thought suddenly. The boy was at least sixteen, because he had a driver's licence. He had a nice smile and merry eyes – greenish-grey eyes. He had brown hair with a dip in it. He was not really tall, but he was tall enough so a medium-sized girl could wear heels and not feel she had to scrooch down when she walked beside him. He was outdoors a lot, because he was so tanned, and he must be new in Woodmont, because she had never seen him before. He looked like a nice boy, full of fun and – best of all – when he saw she was having trouble with Sandra, he understood. One might say they spoke the same language!

But what good does it do me, Jane thought sadly. This was the kind of luck she always had. The boy was sixteen, and nice and understanding, but she didn't even know his name or where he went to school or what town he lived in. But there must be some way she could find out. She didn't know how, but there must be a way. And she was going to find out.

Jane glanced once more at Sandra to make sure she was sleeping soundly. Then she tiptoed out of the bedroom to clean up the ashes Sandra had dumped on the carpet and to let the flies out of the snapdragons.

CHAPTER

2

'Pop, have you ever thought about getting a dog?' Jane asked that evening, after baby-sitting with Sandra and meeting so briefly the boy who delivered horse meat for the Doggie Diner.

'Can't say that I have,' answered Mr Purdy from behind the evening paper. From time to time he stroked Sir Puss, the large tabby cat that was stretched out on his lap. Meticulously Sir Puss licked a paw and scrubbed it behind his ear. When Jane spoke he paused to stare at her disapprovingly for a long moment before he resumed his routine of licking and scrubbing.

That cat acts as if he understood what I said and knew what I was planning, Jane thought. 'Well, don't you think it would be a good idea to have a dog?' she asked.

'What for?' Mr Purdy asked.

'For a watchdog,' Jane suggested.

'In Woodmont?' Mr Purdy lowered the paper and looked at his daughter through a cloud of pipe smoke. 'Nobody even bothers to lock doors in Woodmont. I don't know what we would want a watchdog for.' He raised the paper again as if that ended the discussion.

'Dogs are nice pets,' Jane persisted. 'Lots of people keep dogs just because they like them.'

'We have a nice pet.' Mr Purdy dropped one half the paper to pet Sir Puss, who rested his chin on his master's knee and closed his eyes with a look of self-satisfaction on his tiger face.

'But dogs are different,' said Jane. 'They are loyal and faithful and –'

'Yes, I know,' Mr Purdy interrupted. 'I've read about what noble animals dogs are too. Man's best friend and all that. They rouse sleeping people in burning buildings. They drag little children out of fish ponds. They also dig up gardens. I have enough trouble with the neighbours' dogs running through the begonias and burying bones in the chrysanthemum bed without spending perfectly good money on a four-legged force of destruction of our own.'

'We can get a dog free at the dogs' home,' Jane argued. 'We wouldn't have to spend money on a fancy dog with a pedigree and everything. We could just drive over and pick out a nice plain dog that needs a good home.' As far as Jane was concerned, the only qualification a Purdy dog needed was a good appetite.

Mr Purdy rubbed his cat under the chin. 'Now take Sir Puss, here,' he said. 'There's a pet for you. The handsomest cat and the best gopher hunter in Woodmont. And he wouldn't stand for a dog. He would run a dog off the place.'

'Some cats get along with dogs,' Jane pointed out.

'Not Sir Puss,' said Mr Purdy. 'He's too old and set in his ways.'

'And I don't like to think what life would be like if I had to let a dog in and out, in and out, all day, too. Sir Puss keeps me busy enough opening doors,' said Jane's mother. 'Jane, why this sudden interest in a dog? You've never mentioned one before.'

'Oh, I don't know,' answered Jane vaguely. 'I just thought a dog might be nice to have around.' Well, that took care of that. Neither her father nor her mother would consent to a dog, so there was no chance of the Purdys' having horse meat delivered by the Doggie Diner. And no chance of her getting to know the strange boy that way. She would have to think of some other way. And she must think of it soon. If he had recently moved to Woodmont and would be entering Woodmont High in September, it would be a good idea to get to know him before school started and all the girls saw how attractive he was. Half a dozen girls had probably seen him already and were wondering how they could meet him – girls who were smooth like Marcy. Or maybe they had met him already. And how could a girl meet a boy who delivered food for dogs if her father wouldn't keep a dog?

Sir Puss yawned and stretched luxuriously on Mr Purdy's lap. It seemed to Jane that she had never seen a cat look so self-satisfied. She had loved him since he was a kitten and she was only four years old; she and Sir Puss had grown up together, but at the moment she felt a twinge of annoyance at him for spoiling her plan. As she sat watching the cat settle himself for a nap, she turned her problem over in her mind. The delivery of horse meat had seemed like such a good answer until the cat spoiled it.

Jane watched Sir Puss twitch one ear in his sleep, and suddenly the sight of the well-fed cat gave her an inspiration. 'Say, Pop,' she said, trying not to sound too eager, 'I saw an ad in the paper that said the Doggie Diner delivered horse meat for pets. Wouldn't it be easier to have horse meat delivered for Sir Puss than to get lamb liver from the market? The delivery boy could walk right in and leave it in the refrigerator.'

'Goodness, Jane,' exclaimed Mrs Purdy. 'I wouldn't want to keep horse meat in the refrigerator with our food.'

'And Sir Puss likes liver,' Mr Purdy added. 'He wouldn't eat horse meat.'

'His food is no trouble. I always buy his liver when I get our meat.' Mrs Purdy looked curiously at her daughter. 'You've never taken an interest in the cat's diet before. What's come over you tonight?'

Another good idea that would not work. 'Oh, nothing. I just saw this ad and got to thinking,' said Jane, realizing that she had better be careful what she said, or her mother would start asking a lot of tiresome questions like who was the boy's family and what did his father do and a lot of things she couldn't answer until she got to know him. If only she knew the boy's name she could look him up in the telephone book and just happen to walk by his house, and he might just happen to be outside washing the car or mowing the lawn or something. She would glance at him with a faintly puzzled expression as if she had seen him someplace but couldn't quite remember where. And he would look up from whatever he was doing and say, 'Why, hello. Aren't you the girl who was baby-sitting at the Nortons'?' And she would say ... But she did not know his name and even if she did, he was probably so new in town that his family would not be listed in the telephone directory yet. Or he might not even live in Woodmont. He might live in some other town and when school started he would be part of the school-bus crowd.

Or she could find out where the Doggie Diner was located and just happen to walk past about the time he might be through work. Jane considered this idea and discarded it as being too obvious. A business that cut up horse meat would not be in a part of town where she could go for a walk without having people wonder what she was doing there.

Or she could happen to walk by the Nortons' house about three o'clock on Friday afternoon when he might be delivering Cuthbert's food again. Jane thought this over and decided the plan had both advantages and disadvantages. She could easily go for a walk in the Nortons' neighbourhood without looking out of place. However, the truck probably would not arrive at exactly three o'clock and she could not very well walk up and down in front of the Nortons' as if she were picketing their house. The neighbours would begin to wonder what she was doing. Nevertheless, a leisurely stroll up their street next Friday afternoon could do no harm. He might happen to drive by and see her and think, Why, there's that girl I spoke to at the Nortons'. He would stop the truck and say, 'Hi there. Going to Sandra's house? If you are I'll give you a lift.' And she would say . . .

And then Jane had an even better idea. If she were baby-sitting with Sandra she would be sure to see him. She turned this over in her mind. Could she stand another afternoon of Sandra – another afternoon of trying to manoeuvre her into doing what she was supposed to do when Sandra was so clever at outwitting sitters? To see that boy again, yes. It would not be easy but she could do it. The boy would arrive with Cuthbert's food and say, 'Hi! I didn't expect to see you here again,' and of course he would look as if he were glad she was there again. And she would laugh and say . . .

Jane realized there was another reason for wanting to sit with Sandra Friday afternoons – she might keep some other baby-sitter from meeting the boy.

'Well, I guess I'll phone Julie,' Jane remarked casually.

'Don't talk all night,' said Mr Purdy.

Jane kicked off her shoes and dialled Julie's number. 'Hi, it's me,' she said, when Julie answered. Jane could picture her friend at the other end of the line with her shoes kicked off, too, and her freckled face smiling expectantly. 'Look, Julie, if Mrs Norton wants somebody to sit with Sandra again next Friday, I've got dibs.'

'Jane!' shrieked Julie into the telephone. 'Have you lost your mind?'

'I don't think so,' answered Jane. 'Not yet, anyway.'

'What happened?' Julie asked. 'Has Sandra reformed or something?'

'Lots of things happened.' Jane pulled her knees up under her chin and prepared to make certain no one else would sit with Sandra. 'She shut up a lot of flies in snapdragons and let Cuthbert out when he had just been washed and she dumped an ash tray on the carpet and she threatened to pour ink all over the living-room floor and –'

'That's enough,' cried Julie. 'You can have her any time Mrs Norton wants a sitter, but I still think you're crazy. Or did Mrs Norton pay double or something?'

'No, she paid the usual,' answered Jane. 'And for once she had the right change.'

There was a moment of silence at Julie's end of the line. 'Then there must be a boy in it someplace,' announced Julie. 'There can't be any other reason.'

'At Sandra's? How could there be?' Jane made her voice sound innocent.

'There must be,' insisted Julie. 'There can't be any other reason why, of your own free will, you would offer to sit with Sandra.'

'Have you ever seen a boy there?' asked Jane.

'Jane!' Mr Purdy's voice was warning her that she had talked long enough.

That was the trouble with this house. A girl couldn't even carry on a telephone conversation with any privacy. 'Well, I have to say good-bye now,' Jane said hastily. 'Pop is beginning to bellow.'

'Yes, I know how it is.' Julie's voice was sympathetic. Then she added insistently, 'It must be a boy, but if he's worth an afternoon of Sandra I wish you luck.'

'I'll call you tomorrow. 'Bye.' Jane was glad to hang up. She was willing to share her secret with her best friend, but she did not want to discuss the new boy in front of her mother and father, who would be sure to ask a lot of questions about him that she could not answer. And, on second thought, she did not really want to discuss him with Julie. Not yet. Not until she had a date with him. Jane sat staring at the telephone, deep in her thoughts of the strange boy, until she heard her mother speak to her father.

'I'm so glad Jane is interested in baby-sitting.' Mrs Purdy spoke softly, apparently unaware that her daughter was listening.

If Mom only knew, thought Jane, with a twinge of guilt.

'So many girls her age are boy-crazy,' Mrs Purdy continued. 'Like Marcy Stokes. I don't know what has come over that girl in the past year. She used to be such a good student and now all she thinks about is boys and clothes.'

Well, I know what has come over Marcy, Jane thought. She no longer wears bands on her teeth and she has a figure and a definite personality. She's tall and slim, casual and just a touch bored, with sun-streaked hair and exactly the right clothes. The kind of girl all the boys go for. The cashmere-sweater type. But this, Jane knew, was something she could never explain to her mother, who would say, 'But Jane, you have a cashmere sweater.'

Mrs Purdy went on in a voice so low that Jane had to strain to catch her words. 'I'm glad our daughter is a sweet, sensible girl.'

Mom, how could you, thought Jane. Sweet and *sensible* – how perfectly awful. Nobody wanted to be sweet and sensible, at least not a girl in high school. Jane hoped her mother would not spread it around Woodmont that she thought her daughter was sweet and sensible.

The telephone at Jane's elbow rang so unexpectedly that she jumped before she was able to pick up the receiver. 'Hello,' she said almost absentmindedly, because her thoughts had drifted back to the strange boy who had smiled at her across the Nortons' kitchen.

'Uh ... is this Jane Purdy?' asked a voice – a boy's voice.

An electric feeling flashed through Jane clear to her finger tips. The boy! It was *his* voice! She was sitting there thinking and wishing, and suddenly there he was, on the other end of the line. *He* was calling *her*! Jane swallowed. (Careful, Jane, don't be too eager.) 'Yes, it is.' Somehow she managed to keep her voice calm. To think that she and this boy she wanted so much to know were

30

connected with each other by telephone wires strung on poles along the streets and over the trees of Woodmont! It was a miracle, a real miracle.

'Well, uh . . . I don't know whether you remember me or not, but I delivered some horse meat to the Nortons' when you were sitting with Sandra. My name is Stan Crandall.'

Stan Crandall. *Stan Crandall!* 'Yes?' Ah, good girl, Jane. Calm, polite, just the faintest touch of surprise in her voice. 'Yes, I remember.'

'I called Mrs Norton and asked her for the name of her sitter,' the boy explained.

Oh. Oh, dear. Hang on to yourself, Jane. Maybe his mother is looking for a sitter for his little sister. And what if his mother is looking for a sitter? I'd get to see him, wouldn't I?

'I know this is probably sort of sudden.' The boy hesitated. 'But I was wondering if you would care to go to the movies with me tomorrow night.'

He didn't want a sitter. He wanted her! Jane's thoughts spun. She had better ask her mother. No, that would lead to a lot of tiresome arguments about just who was this Stan Crandall. She couldn't keep him dangling on the telephone while she tried to explain to her mother and father. Besides, she was practically sixteen, wasn't she? She couldn't be tied to her mother's apron strings forever, could she? She had a right to accept a date with a perfectly nice boy, didn't she?

'I would love to go,' said Jane.

'Swell.' There was relief in the boy's – in Stan's – voice. He had been afraid she might turn him down! 'Would seven o'clock be all right?' he asked.

'Seven would be fine,' answered Jane.

'Swell,' he repeated. 'I'll see you then.'

'All right,' agreed Jane, and hesitated. She felt she should say something more, but she could not think what. There did not seem to be anything more to add to the conversation. 'Good-bye,' she said. 'Thank you for calling.'

'Good-bye,' he said, 'and thanks a lot.'

Once more Jane sat staring at the telephone. This time she was filled with a confidence that was new to her. Stan Crandall. Stanley Crandall. He liked her! He had seen her once, and even though she had been rumpled and grass-stained and having a terrible time with Sandra, he liked her well enough to go to the trouble of finding out her name and calling to ask her to go to the movies. Jane smiled at the telephone and gave a sigh of pure happiness. *Stan Crandall!*

'Jane, what were you saying about seven o'clock?' Mrs Purdy called from the living-room.

Jane stopped smiling. Here it comes, she thought. She might as well get it over. Her mother and father would *have* to let her go. They had to. She couldn't bear it if they wouldn't. Jane walked into the living-room determined to be firm with her mother and father and said, as calmly as she could, 'I'm going to the movies tomorrow night at seven o'clock.'

'With some of the girls?' asked Mrs Purdy.

'No. I'm going with a boy named Stanley Crandall.' Jane tried unsuccessfully to keep a note of defiance out of her voice.

Mr Purdy put down the seed catalogue he was studying. 'And who is Stanley Crandall?' he demanded.

'Yes, Jane,' said Mrs Purdy. 'Just who is this Stanley Crandall?'

Oh, Mom, do you have to refer to him as 'this Stanley Crandall'? Jane thought. It sounded so awful, as if she had picked him up on a street corner someplace. 'He's a perfectly nice boy,' she said.

'Where did you meet him?' inquired Mrs Purdy.

'At the Nortons',' replied Jane.

'Is he a friend of theirs?' persisted Mrs Purdy.

'Not exactly. At least I don't think so.'

'Then how did you happen to meet him at the Nortons'?'

Oh, Mom, do you have to act like the FBI, or something, just because I'm going to the movies tomorrow night with a perfectly nice boy, Jane thought. 'He came in a delivery truck,' she said.

'From Jake's Market?'

Jane stared at the corner of the living-room ceiling. 'No. Not from Jake's Market,' she said patiently.

'Jane Purdy!' said Mrs Purdy sharply. 'Will you please get that look of exaggerated patience off your face? Your father and I are not morons. We only want to know for your own good who this boy is.'

Her own good. Everything around here was always for her own good. Well, they would have to know the truth some time. 'He was delivering horse meat for the dog from the Doggie Diner.'

Mr Purdy gave a snort of laughter. 'Aha! Horse meat!' he exclaimed. 'The plot thickens!'

Jane tried to wither her father with a glance but succeeded only in giving him a look of despair. How could he be so callous when she was in the middle of a crisis?

'Really, Jane,' said Mrs Purdy weakly. 'Horse meat!'

'And what's the matter with horse meat?' cried Jane. 'Delivering horse meat is a perfectly honest way for a boy to earn some money. It's no worse than baby-sitting. You always said honest labour was nothing to be ashamed of.' Jane stared defiantly at her mother and father. 'You just don't want me to have any fun!' Jane knew when she said this that it was not true. Her mother and father were both anxious for her to have a good time, but somehow this was the sort of thing she had found herself saying to them lately. She was sorry, but honestly, the way a girl's mother and father could take a beautiful feeling of happiness and practically trample it in the dust!

'We're not forbidding the banns just because the boy delivers horse meat,' said Mr Purdy mildly, as he lit his pipe and flicked out the match.

'Oh, Pop,' said Jane impatiently. 'I don't want to marry him. I merely want to go to the movies with him.'

'Horse meat!' Mrs Purdy began to laugh. 'He delivers horse meat!'

Jane turned on her mother and said almost tearfully, 'It's U. S. government-inspected horse meat!'

'I'm sorry, Jane.' Mrs Purdy managed to stop laughing. 'There is no reason for you to get so worked up. It isn't the quality of the horse meat that we are questioning. We only want to know something about the boy. Surely that's not too much to ask.'

'Well, he's new in Woodmont,' said Jane, somewhat mollified, although still ruffled because her mother had laughed at a perfectly honest way for a boy to earn some money. 'And he's an awfully nice boy.'

'But Jane, how do you know he's a nice boy?' Mrs

Purdy asked. 'You never saw him before. You don't know his family or anything about him except that he delivers horse meat. That isn't much of a recommendation.'

How could she explain to her mother that because a boy had a dip in his hair and a friendly grin and wore a clean white T-shirt she knew he was a nice boy? 'He just is,' was all Jane would say miserably. 'I can tell. And anyway, I'm going out with him, not his family.'

Mrs Purdy did not look convinced, so Jane went on. 'He's not the type to ride around in a hot rod and throw beer cans out along the highway. Mom, I *know* he's a nice boy. He looks clean and intelligent and – well, *nice*. And he looks like he's fun to be with, too. Not like the boys I've known all my life. Not like George, who just thinks about his old rock collection and chemistry experiments.

'Now, Jane,' said Mrs Purdy, 'don't underestimate George. He's a nice boy with real interests. He may not seem very exciting to you now, but he's the kind of boy with a purpose, the kind of boy who will be a doctor or a scientist when he grows up.'

'But Mom, I don't want to go out with a boy I have known practically since I was in my play pen, and I don't care what George is like when he grows up. I want to go to the movies on Saturday night with a boy who is fun *now*.'

'Why, Jane,' Mrs Purdy protested. 'You've always had a good time at the little dancing parties you have gone to.'

'Little dancing parties! Mom, those are for children.'

'And you have gone to the movies and school affairs with George,' Mrs Purdy pointed out. 'I thought you liked him.'

'I do like George,' Jane insisted. 'I just don't like to go

35

out with him. He's too short and that lock of hair always sticks up. At the spring dance at school all he talked about was his rock collection, and he's a horrible dancer. He sort of lopes around and I had to scrooch down so I wouldn't tower over him. And his mother and father came to pick us up, because he isn't old enough to have a driver's licence and they came early because they wanted to *watch* the dance, and it was just too embarrassing, and then when they were leaving the gym his mother said to his father in a loud voice, "Wasn't it a lovely party for the children?" Everybody looked at George and me and I felt about six years old and it was simply ghastly. *That's* why I don't like to go out with George.'

'Oh,' said Mr Purdy. 'I see.'

Jane looked quickly at her father to see if he was laughing at her, but his expression was serious.

'I suppose it was a little awkward,' said Mrs Purdy, 'but just the same, I don't want you running around with a boy we know nothing about.'

'But I'm not going to run around with him. I'm going to walk five blocks in a straight line with him to the movies. That isn't running around.'

Then Jane's father spoke up. 'I think that by now Jane is old enough to recognize a nice boy when she sees one. And as she has pointed out, they are only going to the movies.'

Jane looked gratefully at her father. Good for Pop! He understood.

'But she's had so little experience,' protested Mrs Purdy.

Experience! How was a girl going to get any experience when her mother was so old-fashioned she didn't even want her daughter to go to the movies with a boy unless she personally knew his whole family tree for a couple of generations?

'Does this boy have a car?' Mrs Purdy asked.

'I don't know,' answered Jane truthfully, fervently hoping that he did own a car or at least have the use of one.

'It's all right if you walk to the movies,' said Mrs Purdy, 'but I don't want you riding around in a car with some strange boy.'

'Yes, Mom.' The battle was won, although somehow Jane had known from the beginning that she would win. She was actually going to the movies with Stan, the new boy, the boy with the friendly smile and the dip in his hair. In less than twenty-four hours she would be with him. The problem of the car she would meet when she came to it. If Stan did arrive in a car, she could easily suggest that since it was a nice evening (and it would be a nice evening, it had to be), they could walk to the movies. The cinema was only five blocks from her house, and in the meantime her mother and father would see for themselves what a nice boy he was and maybe the next time . . .

There has to be a next time, thought Jane, as she curled up in a chair with a book in her hand. I couldn't bear it if there isn't another date. And another and another. She saw herself chattering with a cluster of girls in front of the lockers at Woodmont High. 'Stan and I had the most wonderful time . . .' 'Last night Stan and I . . .' 'And Stan said to me . . .' 'Oh, yes, Stan gave me this . . .' (Gave her what? An identification bracelet? His class ring?) 'Stan dropped over last night and we . . .' 'I thought I'd die laughing when Stan . . .'

'Jane, hadn't you better think about going to bed?' Mrs Purdy asked.

Her mother's voice scarcely touched Jane's thoughts. Still standing by the lockers at Woodmont High, Jane answered, 'I guess so,' and walked dreamily toward the bathroom to start putting her hair up in pin curls. 'Stan and I always . . .' 'Stan and I . . .'

CHAPTER

3

IT was not until the next morning that Jane began to have qualms about her date with Stan Crandall. First of all, she decided that her hair simply would not do, so she washed it and put it up in pin curls, each one clamped with two bobby pins.

'Why, Jane, I thought you washed your hair day before yesterday,' remarked Mrs Purdy.

'Did I? I don't remember,' fibbed Jane, staring critically at herself in the mirror. Carefully she plucked six hairs out of her left eyebrow and five out of her right.

Then she opened her closet and studied her wardrobe to see what she owned that would be suitable to wear to walk five blocks to Woodmont's only movie and perhaps to Nibley's afterwards. One by one she examined her dresses. Her best navy-blue silk printed with white daisies was too dressy. Her grey suit – well, no. That was more for wearing to the city. Her pale-blue princess dress – certainly not. Not that old thing. Her yellow cotton – no. Stan had already seen it. Besides, the round collar looked so babyish. Her dirndl and peasant blouse wouldn't do either. Once more she went over her wardrobe. She did not have a thing that was exactly right to wear on her first date with Stan Crandall. Not one single thing – and neither did she have enough money from baby-sitting to buy a new dress.

Jane decided to approach her mother. 'Mom, if I give you six dollars and a half baby-sitting money that I have, could I charge a dress and pay you the rest later?' she asked.

'Why, Jane, you have a closet full of clothes. More than lots of girls in Woodmont.'

This was the sort of thing Jane might have expected from her mother. 'Well, may I, Mom? I haven't a thing to wear tonight.'

'I don't think so, dear.' Mrs Purdy was pleasant but definite. 'There are lots of girls who would be glad to have your pretty clothes. Besides, you are only going to walk five blocks to the neighbourhood movie.'

That was Mom, always dragging 'lots of girls' into arguments. And you'd think she could understand how important those five blocks were. 'But, Mom –'

'Jane,' sighed Mrs Purdy, 'I don't know what's come over you. It wasn't so long ago that I had a terrible time getting you out of play clothes and sneakers.'

And now that I want to dress up, you won't let me charge anything, thought Jane, and it was her turn to sigh. Sometimes she, too, wondered what had come over her.

Jane spent half an hour pressing her blue princess dress and suffering qualms about herself. What would she say to Stan? She could ask him how long he had lived in Woodmont and where he had lived before. That would take up part of the time, but what could she talk about after that? The Teen-Age Corner in the newspaper advised girls to ask questions about boys' interests, but she couldn't come right out and say, 'What are you interested in?' If she said, 'Are you interested in sports?' he might turn out to be a Rugby fan or excited about something else she knew nothing about. Maybe she had better start reading the sport sections after this. And if he did take her to Nibley's, would she know how to act? Going there in the evening with a boy was not the same as dropping in with Julie after school.

Cleaning her white Capezio slippers and painting her nails with Rosy Rapture polish took a good part of the afternoon. It was not until nearly three o'clock, as she wafted her damp finger tips back and forth to dry them, that Jane began to have qualms about Stan. What if he came in a T-shirt and jeans? Or one of those gaudy sports shirts with the tail hanging out? A plain sports shirt with the tail tucked in would be all right for a movie date in Woodmont, but not a T-shirt or a figured sports shirt. But he won't, he can't, she thought. He was not that kind of boy. And all at once she was no longer sure what kind of boy Stan was. Maybe he was the kind who would drive up and toot and expect her to come running out – as if her mother would let her. Or maybe he would chew gum and snap it and guffaw at the love scenes in the movie. Maybe he wouldn't know how to talk to her mother and father, or maybe he would walk on the inside of the sidewalk and let her walk beside the kerb. Maybe he would turn out to be like George and buy ice-cream cones to eat on the way home and lick his cone the way George did. Maybe he even had a rock collection like George and, like George, a scientific mind. Maybe she would have to listen to him tell about finding an unusual piece of contorted gneiss in the Sierras. George never picked up rocks that were just pretty. He always found specimens that he called by the exact scientific name.

Then Jane looked around the Purdy living-room and wondered if she should try to get her mother to call in an interior decorator, now that she was going to have dates. She decided against it. The rug was worn by the door and one chair was pretty shabby where Sir Puss insisted on sharpening his claws on it, but the room was pleasant and comfortable.

Just before dinner Jane took the bobby pins out of her hair, because her father did not allow her to come to the table with her hair in pin curls. He said it spoiled his appetite to realize he had a pinhead for a daughter. It was not until she was seated at the table that Jane began to have qualms about her parents. Between bites of salad she considered them with a feeling of great detachment, as if she were seeing them for the first time. On the whole, she found them presentable, but she did wish her mother would put on some stockings and wear a dress instead of that striped cotton skirt and red blouse. It was so undignified for a mother who was practically forty and very old-fashioned to go around with bare legs, even if they were tanned, and to wear such gay clothes. Stan might think she didn't know how to dress. And her father – if only he wouldn't try to be funny when Stan arrived! His jokes were all right for the family, but he should realize that he had been out of college sixteen years and was too old to go around trying to be funny in front of company. Stan's father probably didn't make jokes all the time and Stan might think it was undignified. Jane barely touched the casserole dish, even though it was her favourite – the one her mother called 'It Smells to Heaven.' There were onions in it and Jane did not want to breathe onions on Stan at the movie.

After dinner Jane decided the blue dress would not do at all. It was terrible, and how could she ever have thought she could wear it? She hastily pressed a pink blouse to wear with her suit. As soon as she had it pressed she realized it was all wrong and of course she would have to wear the blue dress. Hurriedly she locked herself in the bathroom, where she took a shower and washed her face carefully with a deep pore cleanser. She examined her face critically in the mirror and plucked one more hair out of her right eyebrow.

'Jane, you aren't the only member of the family who uses the bathroom,' Mrs Purdy reminded her through the bathroom door.

'O.K., Mom.' Jane scurried into her room. She slid the blue dress over her head and slipped into her clean white shoes. It took four attempts to get a straight parting in her hair. Then, with a lipstick brush which she kept hidden from her mother, who was inclined to be old-fashioned about make-up, Jane outlined her lips with Rosy Rapture, which all the girls were wearing this summer. She filled in the outline, studied the effect in the mirror, and then blotted off some of the colour so she could get out of the house without her mother's saying, 'Really, Jane, I do wish you wouldn't wear so much lipstick.' A light dusting of powder on her nose came next. Finally she studied herself carefully and snipped off two wisps of hair with her manicure scissors. Then she was ready.

At five minutes to seven Jane walked into the living-room and looked around with a critical eye. She was pleased to see a bowl of fresh begonias, vivid as flames, on the coffee table. Thank goodness her mother had changed to a dark linen dress and had put on stockings, and her father, who was wearing a plain tan sports shirt, had put on his horn-rimmed glasses to read the evening paper. He looked almost dignified. Even Sir Puss was stretched out on the rug, languidly patting at his rubber mouse with one paw and behaving properly for a cat. Now if they would all stay that way and not move until Stan came, everything would be all right.

'Well, how about it, Jane?' her father asked jovially. 'Do we pass inspection?'

'Pop, just this once, please don't try to be funny,' implored Jane as she sat carefully on the edge of a chair so she would not wrinkle her dress. Her mouth was dry and her hands felt cold. Her thoughts were anxious. In five more minutes . . . he did say tonight, didn't he . . . tonight and not next Saturday? In three more minutes . . . Please, Stan, don't be late! And please, please be as nice as I think you are.

At exactly seven o'clock Jane heard someone coming up the front steps. She had not heard a car stop in front of the house, so that was one problem she would not have to meet this evening.

'Hist!' said Mr Purdy in a stage whisper from behind his paper. 'I hear footsteps approaching.'

'Pop!' begged Jane, starting from her chair even though she had anticipated the sound of the door-bell. Sir Puss jumped up and glared, annoyed at this disturbance of his peace.

Jane opened the door. 'Hello, Stan,' she murmured, suddenly feeling shy. 'Won't you come in?'

'Hello, Jane.' Stan stepped into the living-room. He was even more attractive than Jane remembered. His greenish eyes and the dip in his hair were the same, but he was wearing grey flannel slacks, a white sports shirt, and a green sweater – not cashmere, but a good-looking wool.

44

His manner no longer seemed easy and casual as it had yesterday when he delivered the horse meat. Now he appeared serious, even a little nervous, as if he, too, were not quite sure how this date might turn out. He was a boy any girl would be proud to introduce to her parents.

'Uh ... Mother, may I present Stan Crandall?' said Jane carefully.

'Hello, Stan,' said Mrs Purdy warmly, and Jane was proud of her.

'How do you do, Mrs Purdy?' Stan answered.

The anxiety that had tormented Jane all afternoon now began to fade. 'And Father, this is Stan Crandall.'

Mr Purdy rose from his chair and extended his hand. Stan stepped forward to shake hands and, as Jane watched helplessly, seeing what was about to happen, he trod squarely on Sir Puss's rubber mouse. The mouse gave out a piercing squeak. Stan jumped and turned red to the tips of his ears.

'Oh!' gasped Jane, embarrassed and ashamed that she had not foreseen this. That cat!

Gamely Stan grasped Mr Purdy's hand and said, as if nothing had happened, 'I'm pleased to meet you, sir.'

'Won't you sit down?' invited Mr Purdy. Stan glanced uncertainly at Jane and remained standing.

In her relief that introductions were over, Jane leaned against the end of the sofa. So far so good, in spite of the rubber mouse. Now what happens, she wondered. Should they talk awhile, or should she suggest that they leave, or should she wait for him to suggest it?

Mr Purdy sat down again, but Stan remained standing. 'That's a handsome cat you have,' he remarked.

45

Sir Puss stared balefully at the visitor, then sat down, hoisted his hind leg, and began deliberately to wash.

Inwardly Jane squirmed with embarrassment. Leave it to Sir Puss! You'd think he was the most important member of the family, the way he acted. Why, oh, why did he have to choose this particular moment, when everyone was looking at him, to wash his bottom? And be so industrious about it. Why couldn't he wash his face prettily? And why did Stan have to stand there so awkwardly? Why didn't he sit down?

'Yes, he's a mighty fine cat,' agreed Mr Purdy. 'And he's a good hunter.'

Jane shifted her weight from one foot to the other and wished her father would not get started on Sir Puss. If only Stan would sit down instead of standing there looking so ill at ease. Jane wished desperately she could push him into a chair. He should know better than to stand there when her father had asked him to sit down. Then she caught her mother's eye. Mrs Purdy frowned ever so slightly and looked meaningfully at the place beside her on the sofa. Jane understood the message and, crimson with embarrassment, hastily sat down. Of course she should have realized that a boy with such nice manners as Stan's would not be seated while she was standing. How could she ever have done such an awkward thing? Now Stan would think she didn't know any better. In spite of her humiliation, Jane was tremendously relieved when at last Stan sat down.

'Yes, he's a great cat,' Mr Purdy went on, as if a crisis had not taken place before his eyes. 'He always wants to be praised when he catches a mole. If he can find an open window he will jump into the house with the mole in his mouth. He weighs fourteen pounds and he lands with a thud that wakes up everyone in the house. You might say –'

Pop, implored Jane silently, not that joke. Please, not that old joke. It was all right for the family, but maybe Stan hadn't read the poem about the fog coming on little cat feet. He might not get the point.

'You might say,' Mr Purdy went on, 'that what we need around here is a cat that comes on little fog feet.'

Stan laughed – a natural boyish laugh. In spite of her annoyance with her father, Jane smiled. So Stan had also read the poem in his English I class. That was good to know. It gave them something in common. Now if she could just get her father to stop talking about Sir Puss and keep him from getting started on his begonias, maybe they could go on to the movies. But now that Stan was finally seated, how on earth was she going to get him up again? If she stood up he would probably get to his feet too, but that did not seem the way to do it. Sitting down and standing up had always been such a simple process until now. Suddenly life seemed unbearably complicated.

Not knowing what else to do, Jane smiled timidly across the room at Stan, who seemed to understand. 'Perhaps we should go,' he said, 'if we want to catch the beginning of the movie.'

'Yes, I think we should,' agreed Jane. She rose from the sofa, an act that brought Stan to his feet. She went to the hall closet and pulled her short white coat from a hanger. Another uncomfortable moment came when Stan took the coat from her to help her into it, and her arm missed the left sleeve twice before she groped her way into it. She was sure Stan would think she was not used to having

47

a boy help her on with her coat. And how right he would be!

'Mrs Purdy, is it all right if I have Jane home by ten-thirty?' Stan asked.

Jane could tell her mother was pleased to have Stan ask this question. She herself would have preferred Stan to think she was old enough to come in whenever she wanted to, but on the other hand, if she wanted more dates with him, it was a good idea to please her parents. And it was pleasant to feel protected as long as it was Stan, and not her parents, who was doing the protecting.

'Yes, I think ten-thirty is late enough for her to be out,' said Mrs Purdy. She smiled encouragingly at Stan, while Jane did some rapid mental arithmetic. About two and a half hours for a single feature, cartoon, and newsreel, fifty-five minutes at Nibley's, and five minutes to walk home.

'I'll have her back by then,' Stan promised.

'Have a good time, kids,' said Mr Purdy.

Kids! Pop *would* have to call them kids. Oh, well, thought Jane, what difference did it make? She was starting out on a date with Stan, and he was every bit as nice as she had thought he would be.

'I hope you don't mind walking,' said Stan, when they were outside. 'Dad won't let me have the car very often.'

'It's a lovely evening to walk,' answered Jane. So his father did let him have the car sometimes! 'Have you lived in Woodmont long?'

'A little over a month,' said Stan. 'We lived in the city, but my folks decided to move over here to get out of the fog.'

'We have fog here too,' said Jane, to keep the conversa-

48

tion going. She noticed that Stan walked on the outside of the sidewalk.

'Yes, but not like the fog in the city. It really dripped, out where we lived.'

Jane wanted to find out as much as she could about Stan in the five blocks to the movie. 'Where do you live in Woodmont?' she asked.

'On Poppy Lane,' he said. 'It's sure nice over there. We have an acacia tree in the front yard and a big fig tree in back.'

Poppy Lane. About a mile from the Purdys'; on the other side of the shopping district, but in the same kind of neighbourhood. If the Crandalls had a fig tree in the back yard, their house must be fairly old, like the Purdys', and that meant they were neither very rich nor very poor. Just average. Jane smiled to herself. Things were working out better than she had dared hope.

By the time they reached the Woodmont Cinema, Jane had learned that Stan, besides his younger sister, had one who was two years older than he was and that he would enter his junior year at Woodmont High in September. In the meantime, he had this job working for the Doggie Diner, because his cousin owned the business and because he liked dogs and planned to be a veterinary surgeon when he finished college. He does have a purpose, Jane told herself triumphantly. Conversation was not so difficult, after all, and the five blocks were much too short. Stan was soon pushing his money through the hole in the glass window of the Woodmont Cinema ticket booth.

Afterwards Jane realized she had been too busy turning over in her mind all she had learned about Stan to remember much about the movie they saw together. It began with a schoolmarm getting out of a stagecoach while a lone horseman rode into town, and it ended with a kiss against a Technicolor sky, and in between there was a fight in a saloon, shooting on the street, the sound of horses' hoofs in the night, and something about a mortgage. What Jane did remember clearly were the admiring glances of several Woodmont High girls who had seen them take seats just before the lights were lowered, and Stan's shoulder above hers, and the way their elbows kept bumping accidentally until she folded her hands in her lap. She did not want Stan to think she was the kind of girl who expected to have her hand held just because she was sitting in the dark with a boy.

After the movie Stan said, 'How about stopping at Nibley's? We still have time.'

'O.K.,' agreed Jane happily, and the two walked half a block down the street to Nibley's Confectionery and Soda Fountain. Once inside, Jane could not decide whether it would be better to sit in a booth in the back, where she would be sure to have Stan all to herself, or whether it would be better to sit toward the front, where she could show him off to the rest of the crowd. She nodded and spoke to a boy who had been in her history class, a girl from her gym class, and two more from her registration room, and hoped she was behaving as casually as if she were used to walking into Nibley's with a good-looking boy. The girls spoke to Jane, but they looked at Stan. Jane noticed wistfulness, envy, or just curiosity on their faces – depending, Jane decided, on whether they were with other girls, boys they didn't like much, or dates they really liked. It was, Jane felt, a very satisfactory experience.

Jane was surprised that Stan, who had lived in Woodmont only a month, knew so many people and could call them by name. They couldn't *all* have dogs that ate Doggie Diner horse meat. Stan guided her into the only unoccupied booth, which was toward the front. Jane looked around her at the signs painted on the mirror behind the milk-shake machines and remembered that only yesterday she had imagined herself sitting at the counter catching the eye of some strange boy in that mirror. Now she felt sorry for the girls who were sitting together at the counter sipping cokes and watching the door to see who would come in next. The jukebox began to play *Love Me on Monday*, and Jane watched its colours turn and shift and thought how much they looked like the fruits that boiled in the kettle when her mother made jam. The slow, rolling-boil stage, the cookery books called it. Jane brushed this irrelevant thought out of her mind. She was wasting precious time that she could spend talking to Stan.

'What would you like?' Stan asked, as Mr Nibley himself appeared to take their order.

'Well, hello there, Janey,' said Mr Nibley jovially. 'Aren't you out pretty late?'

Jane smiled weakly. Oh, Mr Nibley, she thought desperately, *don't*. Don't let Stan know I don't come in here with boys after the movies all the time. That was the trouble with a town like Woodmont. Everyone in the older part knew everything about everyone else. Mr Nibley had known her since she had to be lifted on to a stool and he had to lean over to hand her an ice-cream cone. He probably thought she was about eleven years old now.

As Stan asked for a chocolate shake, Jane found she was too excited to eat. 'A dish of vanilla ice-cream,' she said

51

at last. Tonight a chocolate soda seemed too childish to order.

'Why, Janey, what's the matter?' asked Mr Nibley. 'Don't you like chocolate soda any more?'

'I don't feel like one tonight,' Jane said aloud. In her thoughts she was saying, Mr Nibley, did you *have* to go and tell Stan what I usually order? And please go away. I want to talk to him.

'Say, Janey, I just happened to think,' Mr Nibley said. 'Do you happen to know what kind of fertilizer your father is using on his begonias this year? I don't seem to get the same results he does.'

Fertilizer for begonias! 'No, I don't, Mr Nibley. I never noticed,' answered Jane. Go away, Mr Nibley, she thought. *Go away.*

But when Mr Nibley did leave, Jane found she did not know what to say. Talking to Stan when she faced him in the light was much more difficult than talking while walking beside him in the dusk. She smiled across at Stan, who smiled back at her. Jane glanced down at the initials scratched in the paint on the table and raised her eyes again. How smooth and tan, almost golden, his skin looked. It was funny she had not noticed before that his eyelashes were thick and the crest of the dip in his hair was faded to a light brown. And on his right wrist – a strong-looking wrist – was a silver identification bracelet. Maybe some day . . .

'You were having quite a time with Sandra when I first saw you,' Stan remarked.

Jane laughed. 'Perfectly awful. You saved my life. I don't know what I would have done if she had really dumped that ink all over the carpet.' This was better.

Feeling more at ease, Jane told Stan about her experience with Sandra and the fly spray.

Stan was amused. 'Mrs Norton has just as much trouble with Sandra herself,' he said. 'Do you baby-sit often?'

'Once or twice a week,' Jane explained. 'My friend Julie and I have built up a sort of business.' She did not mind telling this to Stan, because he had a part-time job himself. There were some boys at Woodmont High who would look down on a girl who baby-sat regularly.

Mr Nibley set the vanilla ice-cream down in front of Jane and, by not looking up, she managed to avoid conversation with him. She took a small bite of ice-cream and looked across at Stan, who was peeling the wrapper off a pair of straws. He looked like a boy who was enjoying his date.

'Well, if it isn't Stan Crandall!' cried a girl's voice, and Jane, looking up, saw Marcy Stokes and Greg.

Wouldn't you know it, thought Jane. Marcy *would* have to come along now, when everything was going so smoothly. And at the same time her mind recorded the fact that Marcy already knew Stan. Leave it to Marcy.

'Oh, hello there, Jane,' exclaimed Marcy, with a note of surprise in her voice that made Jane feel as if she were the last person in the world Marcy expected to see at Nibley's with a boy.

'Hi, Jane,' said Greg. 'Mind if we join you? There aren't any empty booths.'

'Sure. Come on,' said Stan, sliding over in the booth. 'Jane and I will be leaving before long anyway.'

Marcy slipped into the booth beside Jane, and Jane felt that everything about herself was all wrong. Marcy's simple black cotton dress and the white cashmere sweater

53

tossed over her shoulders made Jane, in her pastel dress and white coat, feel prim and all bundled up.

'Just coffee, Mr Nibley,' said Marcy. This made Jane, who was nibbling at her vanilla ice cream, feel like a small girl who was being given a treat. She did not drink coffee. To her it was a bitter beverage that grown-ups – no, that wasn't the word – that older people drank.

Marcy flung back her sun-bleached hair with an impatient gesture and smiled lazily at Stan, as if Jane and Greg were not there. 'We sure had fun at the beach that day, didn't we, Stan?' she asked.

'We sure did,' agreed Stan.

What beach? What day? Jane wondered miserably if Marcy's just-between-us-two smile meant that she had already had a date with Stan.

'Except we ran out of sandwiches,' was Greg's comment. 'Next time you women had better remember you're packing a lunch for men, not boys.'

'Such as?' drawled Marcy.

So Greg had been there too, and at least one other girl. Jane was annoyed with herself for feeling so pleased that Marcy had not been alone with Stan – at least not at the beach. But there might have been other times . . .

Greg smiled across the table at Jane. Encouraged, she smiled back, but he did not say anything that would help her enter the conversation. To hide her discomfort she took small bites of her ice-cream. She could not help comparing Greg with Stan while Marcy chattered on. Greg was taller and better-looking than Stan, and there was something different about him, too. Greg knows everybody likes him, she thought, and he expects them to. He's the student-body-president-in-his-senior-year type. Yes, that was it. And Stan – Stan was every bit as friendly, but somehow he was different. Quieter, maybe. Nobody would expect him to be student-body president. He was just nice. The nicest boy she had ever met.

Jane waited for an opening in the conversation that would give her the opportunity to take part. None came. I might as well not be here, she thought unhappily, while Marcy went on about the sunburn everyone got that day at the beach and the fun they all had playing softball. And if she had been at the beach with the others, she would have been miserable trying to play softball with boys.

And then Jane began to question the success of her date. It seemed to her that she had done everything wrong and now it appeared that Stan was already part of Greg and Marcy's crowd, the crowd that belonged and that made her feel mousy and ill at ease. Sitting beside Greg, Stan seemed older and more sure of himself. He was not the student-body president type but he was the kind of boy who would get elected to things – room representative or even president of the Hi-Y. And she was only a girl who wrote 'My Experiences as a Baby-Sitter' for Manuscript and didn't get elected to anything.

Stan glanced at his watch. 'Well, we'd better go, Jane,' he said, 'if I'm going to get you home by ten-thirty.'

'Oh, too bad,' said Marcy, her glance lingering on Stan as if his having to take Jane home spoiled her evening. ' 'Bye now.'

Stan hurried Jane home so fast there was no chance to talk until they were standing in the dim circle cast by the Purdys' porch light. 'Four seconds to spare,' said Stan, and smiled down at Jane.

Jane looked at him uncertainly. 'I had a wonderful time,' she said hesitantly, and opened the door. Please, Stan, she thought, I like you so much. Say I'll see you again. 'Well . . . good night, Stan.'

'Good night, Jane,' he answered. 'I'll be seeing you.'

Jane stepped inside the house and stood looking at Stan under the porch light. A halo of moths circled the bulb over his head. 'Well, good night,' she repeated, careful to keep wistfulness and disappointment out of her voice. 'I'll be seeing you' could mean anything. Or nothing.

'Good night, Jane,' he said again and, turning, started down the steps.

Jane closed the door behind her. Her date with Stan was over. She had had a good time in a miserable sort of way. She was proud of Stan and to be with him was a pleasure, but she had been so awkward about everything and he had been so assured, as if he were used to taking girls to the movies all the time. She wondered if he had enjoyed the evening at all. That he would be seeing her told her nothing. It could mean Stan planned to ask her for another date, or it could mean he would say, 'Hi,' when he happened to run into her on the street.

Jane switched off the porch light and the lamp her mother had left on in the living-room, and looked out the front window into the night. If only she didn't feel so dreadfully young! She wished so much not to be fifteen – to be old enough to be casual about a boy and to order coffee instead of vanilla ice-cream. Fifteen was such an uncomfortable age to be when she liked a boy like Stan, a boy who knew how to act with her parents and who was trusted with his father's car sometimes. Well, it was probably all over. Now that Stan had seen how young she was, he could not possibly be interested in another date — not when he was used to Marcy's crowd.

Something shadowy moving in the front yard caught Jane's eye. Puzzled, she peered through the darkness until she was able to separate the moving thing from the shrubs and tree shadows. It was Stan. Stan was still in the front yard! He appeared to be struggling with something in the fire-thorn bushes on the other side of the steps. The street light, obscured by trees, was so dim that she could not see what he was doing. What can he be doing, she wondered, and gasped in disbelief when Stan moved out on to the lawn and she was able to see him more clearly. What she saw could not really be taking place. But there it was. Stan was wheeling a bicycle which he had freed from the thorny shrubs. Now he mounted it and pedalled down the street in the direction of Poppy Lane. Jane stood staring after him; when he turned the corner she could hear him whistling *Love Me on Monday*. A bicycle! Stan had ridden a bicycle over to her house.

When Jane had partially recovered from her astonishment she suddenly saw the whole evening in an entirely different light. A boy who rode a bicycle to a girl's house and hid it in the shrubbery while he took her to the movies could not be so sure of himself, after all. Probably he had to be in early too, and had bicycled over to save time, and had worried about the Purdys seeing him before he had the bicycle out of sight. And when he was out of sight he had begun to whistle *Love Me on Monday*, the song Nibley's jukebox had played, so he was happy when he left her. Maybe he was even thinking about her.

A lot of things about the evening came back to Jane — Stan's nervous look when she had opened the front door, his crimson ears (such nice flat ears) when he stepped on the cat's rubber mouse. Maybe the reason she had trouble finding her left coat sleeve was that he was not used to helping a girl on with her coat. And as for Marcy's crowd, Stan had not lived in Woodmont long enough to know who belonged and who did not. He was friendly to everyone. Well, thought Jane. Well! Things looked different now, and all because of a bicycle.

'Jane?' Mrs Purdy's voice sounded anxious as she opened the hall door.

'Yes, Mom?' answered Jane, turning from the window.

'Did you have a good time, dear?'

'Yes, Mom,' answered Jane. 'A wonderful time.'

Mrs Purdy stepped into the living-room in her bath-robe. 'He seemed like a very nice boy. Did he ask you for another date?'

'No,' answered Jane, and smiled out into the night in the direction of Poppy Lane. 'No. Not yet.'

CHAPTER

4

ALL day Sunday Jane drifted around the house in a happy glow, humming *Love Me on Monday* and hovering near the telephone, because she was sure Stan would call. Monday she stopped humming and hated the telephone, because she was sure he would never, never call. Tuesday he called.

'Hello, Jane? This is Stan,' he said, and to Jane he spoke the most welcome words in the world.

'Hello, Stan,' she answered happily.

'I have to go to work in a little while, but I wondered if I could stop by for a few minutes.'

'I'm sorry, Stan,' Jane was forced to say. 'I was just about to leave for a baby-sitting job.' But of course she could not let him get away, not after waiting two long days for his call. 'Could you – could you come over some other time?' she asked.

'Do you have to go far?' Stan asked.

'About eight blocks.'

'Why don't I come now and run you over to your job?' he suggested. 'I have the truck.'

'Oh, that would be wonderful,' said Jane sincerely, because she was going to see him now instead of waiting for another call.

'See you in about two minutes,' said Stan.

'Mom, Stan is going to drive me to my baby-sitting job,' Jane informed her mother when she had hung up.

Then, fearful that her mother might object to this short ride with a boy, she waited through an anxious moment of silence until her mother answered, 'All right, dear.'

Jane flew to her room, combed her hair, decided to change from her yellow dress into a dress Stan had never seen, decided against changing, because she might not have time, and wished her mother were wearing stockings. And all the while she wondered if Stan was coming to ask her for another date.

In a few minutes the red Doggie Diner truck stopped in front of the Purdys' and Stan bounded up the steps.

'Hi, Stan,' Jane called through the open front door. 'I'm ready. 'Bye, Mom.'

'Hello, Stan,' said Mrs Purdy pleasantly.

Good for Mom, thought Jane; she isn't behaving badly at all, even though she isn't wearing stockings. Seated beside Stan in the Doggie Diner truck, Jane found that once more she felt shy, painfully shy. Stan seemed like a stranger, her mouth felt dry, and she couldn't think of a thing to say.

'Where to?' he wanted to know. 'Sandra's again?'

'Not today, thank goodness.' Jane was able to laugh naturally. 'This afternoon it's Joey Dithridge.' She gave an address in Bayaire Estates, the 'no-down-payment' side of town, and Stan started the truck. Jane felt a thrill of pleasure just to be riding beside him. Of course, the Doggie Diner truck, with the back filled with packages of horse meat, wasn't exactly the same as a convertible, but since Stan was the driver she did not care.

'Is Joey as bad as Sandra?' Stan asked.

'No, Joey's different,' said Jane. 'He's medium-hard to sit with, but not like Sandra. It's just that he's three years old and into everything, so he takes a lot of chasing. His mother doesn't keep anything around that he can hurt, and that helps. She's not like some mothers, who can't make their own children mind but expect a sitter to be able to. I just have to keep pulling him out of drawers and off the backs of chairs and things. Sometimes I can get him interested in trying to fill a shoe box with worms he digs out of the yard with an old tablespoon, and that keeps him busy. Or I can always read him *The Night Before Christmas.*'

Stan laughed. 'In August?'

'Oh, yes,' answered Jane. 'It's his favourite book.'

Stan stopped the truck in front of the Dithridges', one of the new houses in a long row on a straight street. Few of the houses had lawns, but most of them had new shrubs too small to hide the foundations, and every house had at least one tree, two or three feet high, planted in the space that would some day be lawn. On the sidewalk in front of nearly every house was a little wagon or tricycle. Farther on down the street a bulldozer roared and a cement truck rumbled.

Stan turned to Jane and grinned at her. 'I like that yellow dress on you,' he said. 'You were wearing it that day when you were with Sandra, and you looked cute with your hair all mussed up.'

Jane felt herself blush with pleasure. Stan had remembered what she was wearing the first time they met! This was most significant. Now he would surely ask her for a date.

'Hi!' Little Joey Dithridge came running out of the house to meet Jane.

'Thanks a lot, Stan,' she said, reluctantly opening the

61

door of the truck. If they had been riding in a car, she would have waited for him to go around and open the door for her, but riding in a truck was different.

'I'll see you soon.' Stan started the truck. 'Don't let Joey wear you out.'

'Good-bye,' called Jane wistfully, as Joey joyfully tackled her around the knees. 'Hi, Joey.'

'I'm going to chop you up in a million pieces!' cried Joey.

Jane laughed. 'No, you won't,' she answered, 'because I'm bigger and I'll chop you up in a billion pieces first.' This was the way she and Joey always greeted each other. Joey laughed delightedly while Jane absentmindedly pried him loose from her knees. So Stan liked her in the yellow dress! But he had not asked her for another date. He had said he would see her soon. Soon. Jane did not like the word. It could mean anything – an hour or a week or a month. Men were so exasperating.

But Stan did see Jane soon. He saw her the very next day; he came by for a few minutes before he went to work and stayed long enough to drink a coke. Friday evening he telephoned to ask her to go to the movies again on Saturday. When Jane informed her mother and father that she was going to the movies with Stan again, she noticed her father raise his eyebrows ever so slightly, and an expression (could it be disapproval?) crossed her mother's face. They did not object, but Jane was left with a feeling of uneasiness. She hoped they would not start being stuffy and giving her lectures about seeing too much of Stan ('He's a nice boy, but . . .' 'Really, Jane, I think you are a little young . . .') and all that sort of thing – not when everything was going so beautifully. Oh, please,

please don't spoil it all, thought Jane, resolving not to mention Stan so much, even though lately it seemed as if his name was always on the tip of her tongue.

'By the way, Jane,' said Mr Purdy jovially, 'I noticed a mysterious bicycle in the shrubbery that night you and Stan went to the movies. I wonder whose it was.'

'Pop, please don't tease.'

'Tease? Who's teasing?' Mr Purdy asked.

'Pop, promise you won't ever mention the bicycle to Stan,' Jane begged. 'I'm sure he doesn't want me to know he rode it over here.'

'Very mysterious,' said Mr Purdy. 'Very mysterious the ways of the young.'

It was not until Jane and Stan were in Nibley's after the movie that a real problem arose. This time they had a booth to themselves, near the bubbling, boiling jukebox, and Jane did not order a childish dish of ice-cream. She ordered a cup of coffee.

'Do you really like coffee?' Stan asked curiously over his chocolate milk shake.

The coffee tasted bitter. Jane added more cream. 'Sometimes,' fibbed Jane, bravely taking another sip. She felt less sophisticated than she had hoped she would.

'I don't,' said Stan. 'I can't see why so many people like such bitter stuff.'

'Oh, you get used to it,' said Jane, trying to sound convincing. She took another cautious sip.

Someone put a dime in the jukebox, and Stan looked at Jane across the table. 'Next Saturday is the last Saturday of summer vacation,' he said.

'It is, isn't it?' Jane could feel that something special was coming.

'How would you like to go to the city for dinner, with two other couples, to celebrate?' he asked.

Dinner in the city! White tablecloths, courteous waiters, things cooked with mushrooms and herbs, flaming desserts! What on earth would she wear? 'I would love to go,' Jane told Stan, and at the same time she was sure her mother and father would never let her. But they had to, Jane decided. A date for dinner in the city was too important to miss. Jane was filled with a glorious feeling of confidence as she looked across the table at Stan. A boy did not ask a girl to go to dinner in the city unless she was somebody extra-special.

'Greg and Marcy want to go and so does Buzz Bratton, only he hasn't asked a girl yet,' Stan went on.

'It sounds wonderful,' said Jane, although she was disappointed that Marcy was to be included. Buzz Bratton she had known all her life. He was a small, wiry, black-haired boy with a crew-cut, and now that he was a junior in high school Jane classified him as the yell-leader type. When she was in the seventh grade and he was in the eighth he used to wait for her after school on cooking-class day – not to walk home with her, but to chase her and snatch whatever she had cooked and was taking home for her family to sample. After devouring her baked stuffed onion or chocolate cornstarch pudding, he always pretended to have terrible pains in his stomach. However, now that he was older he might be fun on a double date, Jane conceded, if only he didn't tease. A girl shouldn't hold a baked stuffed onion against a boy for ever.

'Dad said I could have the car that night,' Stan continued.

At last they were going someplace in a real car, Jane

thought ecstatically – or rather they were going if her mother and father weren't stuffy and old-fashioned about it. Well, if they were, she would have to talk them out of it. She would plan her campaign carefully.

'We thought it would be fun to have dinner in Chinatown. I used to eat there a lot with my folks when we lived in the city. Do you like Chinese food?'

Jane set down her empty coffee cup and hastily revised her picture of dinner in the city. 'Yes, I do,' she answered, because now that she had managed to get the coffee down, she was sure she would enjoy anything when she was with Stan. She tried to remember if she had ever eaten any Chinese food. Yes – once when she and her mother went shopping in the city they had ordered lunch at a department store tearoom, and chop suey had been on the menu. Or maybe it was chow mein. Anyway, something slithery that Jane did not remember clearly.

That night, after she had watched Stan take his bicycle out of its hiding place in the fire-thorn bushes, Jane lay awake, tense from coffee and excitement. Her thoughts whirled like confetti in the wind – Stan handsome in a white shirt and tie arriving in a car instead of a truck ... riding in the front seat beside Stan ... sitting with him in a Chinese restaurant fragrant with incense (at least she thought a Chinese restaurant would be fragrant with incense; she wasn't sure) ... their eyes meeting across the teacups. The Chinese did drink tea. That she was sure of. How wonderful it was going to be! Now she was really grown-up, mature, sophisticated, a young woman with a dinner date. A dinner date with Stan.

Long after she should have been asleep, Jane's thoughts were interrupted by the peculiar muffled cry of a cat that had been successful in the hunt. Sir Puss had caught another mole, Jane realized, and as she lay listening to his insistent cry she knew he would not be silent until he had received the praise that he felt was his due. Mr Purdy raised his bedroom window, and through her own window Jane caught a glimpse of his flashlight playing on the cat. 'My, that's a big one,' Mr Purdy complimented him and, satisfied, the cat was quiet.

The interruption started Jane's thoughts spinning in another direction. She had to evolve a practical plan for persuading her mother and father to let her go to the city. Sunday breakfast was the best time to bring up the matter, because it might take her all week to win the argument. She would state that she was going to the city for dinner, as if it had never occurred to her that there would be any question about her going. Then she would overcome their objections one by one. 'But Mom, you said yourself he was a nice boy.' 'But Pop, he does drive carefully.' 'But Mom, of course he's a good driver, or his father wouldn't let him take the car.' 'But Mom ...' 'But Pop ...' Over and over again.

On Sunday, however, Jane did not find the right moment to broach the matter to her mother and father. She waited all day, as alert as a cat at a mousehole; but late in the afternoon, when she thought the moment had come and she was about to pounce on it, friends dropped in. They were persuaded to stay for supper and then lingered until Jane had gone to bed.

On Monday Stan called to say that Buzz did not have a date, and did Jane know another girl? After thinking it over, Jane decided to ask Julie, because she felt guilty about having seen so little of her since meeting Stan and because Julie was also fifteen and would not make Jane feel uncomfortable. Jane waited until her mother was out of earshot to telephone Julie and extend the invitation.

'Oh, Jane! Dinner in the city – how marvellous!' Julie squealed with delight. 'Mother and Dad have simply got to let me go!' Julie chattered happily on about how absolutely heavenly it would be to have a date with a boy who wasn't an old family friend, even if he was a little short, and how she was simply mad about Chinese food, especially since it wasn't fattening, and did Jane plan to wear a hat, because if she did Julie didn't know what she would do. Then, after pausing to catch her breath, she asked, 'But Jane, how did you ever talk your family into letting you go?'

Jane sighed. 'I haven't. That's the awful part. I haven't been able to talk to them together yet and anyway, I'm scared to bring it up.'

'I know,' sympathized Julie.

'If your folks will let you go,' said Jane, 'I'm sure mine will let me go.'

'I was thinking the same thing about you,' said Julie.

'Keep me posted,' said Jane, not very hopefully.

'I will,' agreed Julie. 'And phone me the instant you talk them into it.'

Tuesday Julie telephoned. 'Any luck?' she asked guardedly.

'Not yet,' Jane sighed. 'Pop stayed in the city for dinner.'

On Wednesday Julie called just before dinner. Jane knew from the sound of her voice that she did not have good news. 'Tell me, Julie. What happened?' she asked.

'Wouldn't you just know?' said Julie gloomily. 'They're thinking it over.'

'Oh, Julie, how awful,' said Jane. There was nothing worse than having parents think things over.

'Jane, you've simply got to get your folks to say you can go,' Julie begged. 'Then I can use that for an argument.'

'I can't put it off any longer,' Jane admitted. 'Stan doesn't even know they haven't given me permission. He just assumed they would let me go. I guess I'll have to beard them in their dens at dinner tonight.'

'Good luck,' said Julie, not sounding at all hopeful.

And so that evening at the dinner table, when her father was enjoying a second helping of strawberry shortcake, Jane said casually, 'Stan is taking me to the city for dinner Saturday. I think I'll wear my grey suit.' Then she braced herself for the inevitable.

Mrs Purdy set her coffee cup back on its saucer. Mr Purdy laid down his fork. They both looked at Jane.

'Greg and Marcy are going too,' said Jane chattily, as if nothing were wrong. 'And Buzz Bratton will probably take Julie.'

'Jane,' said Mrs Purdy, 'it seems to me that you are seeing a lot of this Stan Crandall.'

Here we go. This Stan Crandall again. 'But Mom, you said yourself he was a nice boy.' There. She had known she could get that in someplace.

'But you are only fifteen,' protested Mrs Purdy. 'I don't think a bunch of fifteen-year-olds should go to the city alone at night.'

Only fifteen! That old argument. Well, she wasn't going to be fifteen all her life. 'I've only been to the movies with him twice and had a couple of cokes with him. I don't think that's seeing such a lot of him. Anyway, except for Julie, I'm the only one who is fifteen. The others are older. Stan must be practically seventeen.'

'Now Jane, I certainly don't want you running around with an older crowd,' said Mrs Purdy.

How unreasonable could parents get, anyway? First Stan and his friends were too young. Now they were too old. 'I don't think sixteen is so awfully much older than fifteen,' Jane pointed out.

'Where do you plan to have dinner?' asked Mr Purdy curiously. 'It seems like a pretty expensive thing for kids that age to be doing.'

'In Chinatown,' answered Jane. 'Stan has eaten there lots of times with his family when he lived in the city.'

'Oh, Chinatown. You get a lot for your money there,' said Mr Purdy. 'The boys ought to be able to fill you up for a dollar or so apiece.'

Jane refrained from asking her father please not to be so crude.

'I just don't like the whole idea,' said Mrs Purdy. 'How do you plan to go? On the bus?'

This was the hardest part. Her mother always got so excited at the thought of her riding in a car with a boy. 'No,' said Jane carefully. 'Mr Crandall is letting Stan have the car.'

'Now Jane,' said Mrs Purdy sharply. 'I am not going to have you running around all over the country in a car with a lot of teen-agers.'

'But Mom,' protested Jane. 'It's less than ten miles to the city. That isn't all over the country. And Greg and Marcy and Buzz and Stan and Julie and I aren't a lot of teen-agers. Except for Stan – and you said yourself he was a nice boy – you've known all of us all our lives.'

'Did Julie's mother say she could go?' Mrs Purdy asked.

'I don't know,' said Jane truthfully, for Julie's mother had not actually refused permission.

'I don't like the whole idea,' said Mrs Purdy. 'You know the sort of things we read about teen-agers in the papers these days.'

'Oh, Mom,' said Jane impatiently, 'you're acting as if we were a bunch of juvenile delinquents. As if we were all out on probation or something.'

'But children your age get into such terrible scrapes,' said Mrs Purdy.

'But not teen-agers like Stan and me,' Jane told her mother, ignoring Mrs Purdy's reference to children. Surely her mother was not going to hold her responsible for every wild teen-age newspaper story she read. 'People like Stan and me don't get into the papers. I told you before I went out with him he wasn't the type to drive around in a hot rod, throwing beer cans around. He's the kind of boy who has a purpose in life, like George. He's going to be a veterinary surgeon when he finishes college.' A purpose in life – that ought to please her mother.

'I think Jane has a point there,' said Mr Purdy. 'It isn't fair to judge all teen-agers by the few we read about in the headlines.'

'I suppose not,' admitted Mrs Purdy, 'but it worries me just the same. I would feel a lot better if they went on the bus.'

Ha! She was gaining ground. This was the first time her mother had admitted the possibility of her going at all. Jane thought quickly. 'But Mom, you know how terrible the bus service is in the evening,' she said. 'After we got to the city we'd have to transfer twice to get to Chinatown. We'd be standing around on street corners all night waiting for buses, and Stan might not be able to get home by ten-thirty.' This was, she admitted to herself, a dangerous argument. It might lead her mother into protests against staying out till all hours. And if she weren't careful, her mother would be dragging in lots of girls. Lots of girls would be satisfied with going to the movies in Woodmont, and that sort of thing.

'I don't see why they wouldn't be safe enough in the Crandalls' car,' said Mr Purdy. 'Stan has lived in the city and is used to city traffic. And he drives a truck, too, so he had to pass the test for a commercial licence. He looks like a pretty steady sort of kid, and if Jane doesn't have any sense now she never will have.'

'I suppose it's all right to let her go just this once,' agreed Mrs Purdy reluctantly. She turned to Jane. 'But you must go straight to Chinatown and come straight home. And be home by ten-thirty.'

'We will,' promised Jane, and thanked her father with one grateful glance across the bowl of begonias in the centre of the table. Darling Pop. He understood. Suddenly hungry because the battle had ended so much sooner than she had dared hope, Jane served herself another piece of strawberry shortcake. She really was going to the city in a car with Stan to have dinner – her first grown-up date. And it was going to be the most wonderful evening she had ever spent in her whole life!

Jane finished her shortcake and hurried to the telephone to dial Julie's number. 'Julie, I can go!' she said ecstatically.

'I was just going to phone you,' answered Julie, equally ecstatic. Her mother and father had finally, *finally* consented to let her go after a lot of talk about teen-agers and speeding and goodness knows what all – you know how parents are.

It did not take more than an hour on the telephone for the girls to decide they would not wear hats, because if they both went bareheaded it wouldn't matter what Marcy did about a hat; that Julie would wear her navy-blue suit, because it made her look thinner, and Jane would wear her grey suit and the white blouse that had tiny tucks down the front and really was very pretty even though it did have one of those awful round collars Mrs Purdy always insisted on. ('But Jane, they're so becoming.' 'But Mom, they're so childish.') Jane would wear her black shoes that looked like pumps except they had low heels, and Julie would try to talk her mother into a new pair of shoes. Both girls would wear, or anyway carry, white gloves, because after all they were going to the city, weren't they? The city was not the same as Woodmont. They had to be well-dressed to go to the city.

'Good heavens, Jane,' Mr Purdy remarked at the end of this conversation. 'You and Julie are only going about eight miles to eat some food you probably won't like, with a couple of high-school kids who are, I would like to remind you, mere mortals.'

Jane smiled vaguely at her father and did not bother to answer. For a fleeting moment she felt sorry for him – poor old Pop, with his cat and his begonias to keep him happy.

Jane spent the rest of the week in joyful anticipation. She was an extra-special girl to Stan, and if her mother and father let her go to the city with him she should have no trouble getting permission for beach picnics and swimming parties. What a wonderful summer this had turned out to be, and fall should be even better. For the first time since she entered Woodmont High she would feel that she really belonged.

Thursday Jane met Julie and although they both had cokes in their refrigerators at home, they walked to Nibley's and ordered cokes. This was a splurge for Julie, who had been dieting for four days and should have ordered tomato juice.

An earnest-looking boy in the front booth was holding the attention of the crowd. 'And so I went up to my counsellor,' he was saying, 'and I said, "Why can't I know what my I.Q. is? After all, it's my I.Q.", and he told me if I found out I had a real low I.Q. of about twenty-seven or something I might get discouraged and quit studying.'

The boy paused, and the two girls exchanged a quick glance. 'I've simply got to find time to wash my hair before we go to the city for dinner with Stan and Buzz,' remarked Julie, in a voice that was not exactly loud but nicely calculated to carry to the crowd around them.

'And my counsellor said if I found out I was a genius I would think I was so good I would quit studying anyhow,' the boy continued, but his audience was losing interest.

'I wish I had a yellow blouse,' said Jane, as if she were completely unaware of the interest others were taking in their conversations. 'Stan always likes me in yellow.'

'So then my counsellor said, "I'll tell you one thing. Your I.Q. is over a hundred," ' the boy went on, but now no one was listening.

The faces reflected in the mirror behind the milk-shake machines revealed that the girls around them were wishing they had dates for dinner in the city too, and that they were sure to spread the news to every girl in Woodmont. Jane and Julie left Nibley's feeling that they had enjoyed an unusually pleasant afternoon.

On Friday Stan came by to drive Jane to a baby-sitting job – an easy job this time, sitting with a baby who slept most of the time and whose mother only went out between feedings and who always left a snack for the sitter. It was really an ideal job and Jane was glad, because she did not want anything to intrude into her lovely glow of anticipation.

'I'm sure glad you can go tomorrow,' said Stan, when it was time for Jane to get out of the truck.

'I'm glad too,' said Jane shyly, hopping to the ground. 'I know we're going to have a wonderful time.'

And the next day was Saturday.

CHAPTER

5

By a quarter to six on Saturday Jane, who had been too excited to eat lunch, was ready. She sat on the edge of the sofa in her carefully pressed suit, pulled on her white gloves, and after a few minutes pulled them off. Then she put them on again, decided they made her feel as if her hands belonged to Minnie Mouse, and peeled them off a second time. Perhaps some day she would learn to wear gloves gracefully.

Promptly at six o'clock the doorbell rang. 'Be still, my heart!' Mr Purdy laid his hand over his heart and spoke in an exaggerated whisper.

'Pop!' implored Jane, as she opened the front door.

Never had Jane seen Stan look so attractive. He had a fresh, scrubbed appearance and was wearing a grey flannel suit, a white shirt that set off his tan, and a green tie, just the right colour for his greenish eyes. Jane stood smiling at him with admiration and sensed at once that something was wrong. Stan was painfully embarrassed.

'Uh ... Jane.' Stan hesitated and then went on. 'At the last minute Dad had to use the car on a business trip, and Greg and Buzz couldn't get their cars either and ... well, my cousin said I could ... uh ... take the Doggie Diner truck. I ... I hope you don't mind going in the truck.'

Jane was engulfed in disappointment. Driving to the city on a special date in a truck, especially the Doggie Diner truck – how perfectly awful! But the expression on

Stan's face quickly made her stifle her own feelings. His eyes were pleading with her not to mind, to be a good sport about riding in the truck.

Jane was filled with sudden sympathy for Stan. She could not let him down. 'Of course I don't mind,' she managed to say gaily. 'What difference does it make? It has four wheels and a motor, doesn't it? That's all that really counts.' Her reward was Stan's smile of relief. Darling Stan. What difference did it make what they rode in, as long as they were together?

When she climbed into the front seat, Jane saw that Greg and Buzz were already sitting on cushions in the back of the truck. Buzz whistled when he saw her. 'Hey, don't you look nice!'

'You're looking sharp yourself,' Jane flashed back at him. It always helped a girl to have a boy whistle at her.

The first stop was Marcy's house, a new house in the hill section of Woodmont. When Marcy walked out to the truck with Greg, she stopped and laughed. 'No!' she exclaimed. 'We aren't really going in the Doggie Diner truck! How perfectly marvellous!'

Out of the corner of her eye Jane could see Stan's face turn red. Shut up, Marcy, she thought fiercely; can't you see Stan is embarrassed enough as it is?

'Isn't this a scream?' Marcy went on, as she climbed into the truck beside Jane. 'Isn't this the funniest thing you ever heard of?'

If it were somebody else who was going to the city in the truck, Jane admitted to herself, she would think it was funny. But since it was Stan who had got them into this situation she could not laugh. She smiled reassuringly at Stan, but his eyes were on the road. Sitting beside him made Jane feel pleasantly possessive and a little important, because her date was the driver. It made up for sharing the seat with Marcy, who was wearing an expensively casual tweed suit with a plain silk blouse and pumps with real high heels. Jane began to feel that her own dainty blouse with tucks and a round collar looked like a baby dress and that her suit was too obviously her best suit. Beside Marcy she felt as prim as . . . well, as prim as Miss Muffet.

The last stop was Julie's house, because Julie lived near the entrance to the freeway. When she came out to the truck with Buzz, Jane saw that she was wearing high heels, which made her taller than Buzz, and that her hands did not look natural in her white gloves. She has the Minnie Mouse look too, thought Jane, and she's wearing a girdle because of her straight skirt. Poor Julie. Unaccustomed to her high heels, Julie turned her ankle, and Buzz caught her by the elbow.

Please, please, Julie, thought Jane, don't make fun of the truck. Don't embarrass Stan. Julie shot Jane a questioning glance. 'Hi, everybody,' was all she said, as she climbed into the back of the truck with Greg and Buzz. Jane relaxed. From now on, in spite of the truck, everything would be as wonderful as they had planned. Suddenly she was hungry, and she remembered that she had skipped lunch.

Jane felt excitement rising within her as the truck left Woodmont and climbed the approach to the bridge that crossed the bay. Through the sunset haze the city at the opposite end of the span looked unreal to Jane. It seemed like an imaginary city, a magic city, a city that had appeared from the mists and might disappear if she closed her eyes for a moment.

'What shall we have to eat?' Buzz asked from the back of the truck. 'Shark's fins?'

'How about carp?' suggested Greg.

Leave it to Buzz to mention food right away, thought Jane, remembering the times he had robbed her of her cooking samples in the seventh grade. Then it occurred to her that goldfish were a kind of carp, but she could not believe they would really have goldfish for dinner. She pictured a platter of fried goldfish garnished with lemon and parsley. It was not an appetizing thought.

'Or fried octopuses,' said Buzz.

'You mean octopi,' corrected Marcy over her shoulder, and everyone laughed. Everyone but Jane. She was beginning to remember reading that the Chinese ate some strange things.

'Anyway, don't you mean squid?' asked Marcy.

'Don't forget bird's-nest soup,' added Stan.

'Ugh!' This was Julie's first contribution to the conversation.

'It's all right.' Greg was comforting. 'They don't use any old bird's nest. They use special birds' nests.'

'How about thousand-year-old eggs?' put in Buzz.

Jane, her appetite diminishing rapidly, suppressed a shudder.

'What's the matter, Jane?' Buzz asked. 'Don't you like eggs that are really ripe?'

'Make mine three-minute eggs,' answered Jane, who had made up her mind not to let Buzz tease her.

'Buzz, you mean hundred-year-old eggs,' corrected Julie. 'And anyway, they aren't really a hundred years old. I had to read a book about China for a book report, and it said the eggs were really only about a hundred days old. They just *call* them hundred-year-old eggs. And they aren't rotten. They are salted or pickled or something. Anyway, the book said they are very good.'

Isn't that just dandy, thought Jane. Only a hundred days old.

'I know what,' said Buzz. 'Let's have flied lice.'

This was too much for Jane. 'They don't really eat lice, do they?' she cried in alarm.

Everyone shouted with laughter. ' "They don't really eat lice, do they?" ' mimicked Buzz, and they all laughed again.

'Don't pay any attention to him,' whispered Stan. 'He thinks he's saying fried rice with a Chinese accent, but I have lots of Chinese friends in the city and I never heard anyone talk that way.'

'Oh.' Jane felt the blood rush to her face. How could she be so stupid? Determined not to be laughed at again, she took a firm grip on her sophistication.

'Which restaurant shall we go to?' Greg asked.

'How about that one on the corner up over the shop with the Chinese furniture?' suggested Marcy.

'That's a tourist trap,' objected Buzz. 'Let's go to a real Chinese restaurant.'

'Yes, one where the Chinese eat,' agreed Stan. 'I know a good one at the end of Chinatown. Hing Sun Yee's.'

'Hey, I know that one.' Buzz sounded enthusiastic. 'I've eaten there several times. It isn't very fancy, but the food is swell.'

'Let's try it,' said Greg.

'Yes, let's.' Jane added a small murmur to the enthusiastic agreement of the others. After all she had heard about bird's-nest soup and hundred-year-old eggs, she secretly thought a restaurant popular with tourists might have been a safer choice. Some of the talk was joking, she knew ; but how much, she could not be sure.

When they reached Chinatown, Stan was unable to find a parking space in the narrow crowded streets. Around and around he drove, uphill and downhill, creeping and stopping, creeping and stopping in the heavy traffic, past a housing project, barber shops, a mortuary, laundries, chair-caning shops, around and around, up and down, creeping and stopping.

When at last Stan spotted a space in front of a hardware store, he said, 'It will be a tight squeeze, but I think I can make it.'

I hope so, thought Jane fervently. Backward and forward Stan manoeuvred the truck, an inch at a time, it seemed to Jane, or even a half inch at a time, until he finally had it parked.

'Let's go. I'm starved,' said Buzz. 'Lead me to that bird's-nest soup.'

Stan led the way down a dingy street unfamiliar to Jane. They passed a herb shop, its walls lined with drawers and its windows filled with glass jars displaying weird-looking specimens. What are those withered things, Jane wondered. Toads, newts, salamanders, pieces of unicorn horn ? Don't be silly, she told herself. They are probably just dried seaweed, or something.

They paused to look at a Chinese grocery with its bundles of thin beans, baskets of flat green peas, a tank of turtles, another of gaping catfish, dishpans full of clams and snails. I won't look, Jane told herself. I just won't look.

A neon sign above the door marked Hing Sun Yee's restaurant. In the window was a row of ducks that had been roasted whole and were now displayed hanging by their heads. As Stan guided Jane into the restaurant, the man at the cash register seized one of the ducks, tossed it on to a chopping block, and hacked it to pieces with a cleaver. Jane hastily looked away. The room, which had a cement floor and a low ceiling, was filled with marble-topped tables. Seated at several of the tables were elderly Chinese men who were wearing hats and eating with chop-sticks.

'Hi, Tom,' Stan said to the young waiter who came forward to meet them. 'How about a booth?'

'Sure,' said Tom. 'Golly, Stan, I haven't seen you for a long time.'

'I live in Woodmont now,' Stan explained. 'We don't get over here very often.'

'We'll sure miss you at school,' Tom said, as he showed them into a booth.

Jane entered first, then Stan, followed by Marcy, who slid into a chair beside him. Jane would have preferred to have Julie sit on the other side of Stan. When they were all seated at the round table, Tom handed them menus and left, pulling a red curtain across the entrance to the booth.

Buzz picked up a cruet filled with brown liquid from the centre of the table. 'Good old beetle juice,' he remarked.

It isn't really beetle juice, Jane told herself. She spread the menu on the marble table top and looked at it in be-wilderment. It was filled with Chinese characters and words that were unfamiliar to her. Chow yuke, fried won ton, polo pai gwat sounded terrible to her. From the chopping block she heard the crunch of little bones. Stop being ridiculous, she said to herself. American dishes like hush puppies or her mother's casserole, 'It Smells to Heaven', would probably sound distasteful to the Chinese. It was only a question of what you were used to.

'Let's each order a dish and then pass them round,' suggested Stan. 'What would you like?' he asked, turning to Jane. He looked so enthusiastic that Jane longed desperately to feel the same way.

'How about some flied lice?' Buzz asked wickedly, his eye on Jane.

Determined not to let the others know how she felt, Jane made a face at Buzz and said, 'I'd like chow mein.'

'Oh, no,' protested Marcy, swinging her blonde hair away from her face. 'Only tourists eat chow mein.'

I guess I said the wrong thing, thought Jane uncomfortably.

'You should get something special here.' Buzz agreed with Marcy. 'You can get chow mein any place.'

'That's all right,' said Stan. 'If Jane likes chow mein, she shall have it.'

Jane smiled gratefully at him. For Stan's sake she must hide her misgivings. She could not let their first big date turn into a disappointment for him.

Tom appeared with six handleless cups and a battered enamel pot filled with tea, which Stan poured while Tom wrote down the orders in Chinese characters. 'Forks or chopsticks?' he asked with a grin.

'Chopsticks,' the boys all said at once. Jane and Julie exchanged an anxious look before Jane bent her head to sip her tea. Good old familiar tea.

Stan held up his cup. 'Here's to next semester.'

'To next semester.' They all raised their cups and drank the toast.

Tom set plates before them and carried in dish after dish of food – bowls of strange sauces, platters heaped with crinkled brown objects, mysterious mixtures of unknown foods. Jane, unable to identify even her own order, glanced across the table at Julie, but Julie did not appear to be worried. Everyone was looking at the bowls and platters with anticipation. Everyone but me, thought Jane miserably. The memory of the herb shop and the produce market floated through her mind. Whacking, crunching sounds came from the chopping block. Jane struggled to subdue her imagination.

'Shrimp roll!' exclaimed Julie. 'I adore it. It's practically my favourite food.'

'Here's your flied lice, Jane.' Buzz handed her a dish.

'Thanks. I can hardly wait.' Jane managed to put a note of gaiety in her voice and helped herself to one spoonful. At least she knew it was rice. That was something. As the dishes were passed around she served herself the smallest possible portions and hoped the others would not notice. One dish, especially strange-looking, made her pause, however. It was a thick red sauce in which floated pieces of onion, green pepper, and what appeared to be tiny brown hands. 'What's this?' she asked lightly, as if she were merely curious.

'Sauce for the won ton,' Greg explained.

'Oh,' said Jane. That did not tell her much. Jane ladled a small spoonful on to her plate. Now if she only knew which was the won ton, and should she pour the sauce over it or dunk the won ton in the sauce? And what on earth could those floating things be that looked like little brown hands?

When everyone was served, Buzz picked up the cruet again and poured some of the soy sauce over his rice. 'Have some beetle juice,' he remarked, as he handed the cruet to Jane.

Telling herself it couldn't really be beetle juice, Jane cautiously poured two drops on her rice. Well, she thought, now I've got to start eating. She watched the others pick up their chopsticks and tried to hold hers the same way. She picked up a few grains of rice, but she could not control the bamboo sticks and the rice dribbled back to her plate. She took a firmer grip and tried to pick up a piece of green pepper from the won ton sauce. It slipped from between the sticks. Telling herself this could not be so difficult – millions of Chinese ate with chopsticks every day, didn't they – she tried again, got a tenuous hold on the pepper, and raised it from her plate toward her mouth. The chopsticks separated and the pepper went sliding down the front of her blouse into her lap.

How awful, Jane thought, as she picked up the pepper with her fingers and slipped it back on to her plate. With her paper napkin she scrubbed at the stain and succeeded only in smearing it through the sheer fabric on to her slip. Miserable, she glanced around to see if the others had noticed. Julie, who had laid down her chopsticks and was surreptitiously tugging at the top of her girdle, cast Jane a glance of sympathy, which Jane returned. Poor Julie, her girdle was cutting into her waist. Buzz and Greg were eating hungrily and Marcy, her sun-bleached hair falling against one cheek, was talking to Stan as if she were alone with him.

84

Jane studied her plate carefully for something familiar that was not dripping with red sauce and that did not look slippery. She settled on what she decided must be the shrimp roll that Julie liked so much. It was made of shredded lettuce, shrimp, and several unknown ingredients covered with a golden crust and cut in bite-sized slices. Concentrating on the shrimp and lettuce and trying not to think what else might be in it, she slipped one chopstick through the crust, bent over her plate, and popped the bit into her mouth. Instantly she was sorry. 'Oh!' she gasped as tears filled her eyes, and she clapped her napkin over her mouth. The shrimp roll was unbearably hot.

'What's the matter?' Stan turned away from Marcy.

Jane gulped and sipped her tepid tea. 'I didn't know it would be so hot,' she said. Because she didn't want to let Stan down, she added bravely, 'It was delicious, though.'

Buzz dipped into the red sauce and held up one of the little brown hands. 'What do you suppose this is?' he asked.

'Sh-h,' giggled Marcy. 'You'll frighten Jane.'

Leave it to Marcy, though Jane bitterly. If she wasn't fooling Marcy she didn't suppose she was making the others think she was having fun, either. How awful could this evening get, anyway? Maybe some day she would look back and laugh and say, 'I'll never forget that awful night a bunch of us had dinner at Hing Sun Yee's in Chinatown.' But this was not some day. It was now and she was miserable. Her head was beginning to ache, she could not enjoy the food and, worst of all, she felt lonely and left out. Stan talked more to Marcy than to her. Not that she blamed him. Nobody could expect a boy to enjoy the company of a girl who hadn't learned to like Chinese food, who couldn't even pretend enthusiasm, and who spilled things all over her clothes like a two-year-old. Her first grown-up date was ruined and probably her friendship with Stan, too.

Buzz grinned at Jane. 'What's the matter, aren't you hungry?' he asked.

Suddenly Jane was piqued with Buzz for teasing her about flied lice and beetle juice. Maybe Stan was losing interest in her, but she was not going to let Buzz get her down any longer. She looked him in the eye and said coolly, 'It's just that your appetite is so big it makes mine look small.'

Buzz seemed taken aback at his failure to get a rise out of Jane, and the others laughed.

Encouraged by Buzz's reaction, Jane went on. 'After all, Buzz, if you could eat my seventh-grade cooking samples, I'm sure you could eat anything, even million-year-old eggs.'

This time everyone laughed at Buzz. 'O.K., Jane, you win this time,' he said, in a way that made Jane wonder how he would try to tease her next.

Somehow Jane got through the rest of the meal. While the others ate heartily, she was able to pick out a few familiar bits from her plate – an almond, a flat green pea pod, a sliver of pork – and convey them unsteadily to her mouth with the chopsticks. She was glad when Tom removed their plates and set down a plate of cookies and brought a fresh pot of tea. The hot drink hurt her burned tongue, but she did not care. The meal was such a dismal failure that nothing mattered any more. There was no use even trying to pretend. She had spoiled Stan's date – the date he had meant to be so special – and he would never ask her for another. She looked sadly at him, as if he had already gone out of her life. Dear Stan, it was nice knowing you, she thought, and it was such fun for a little while until I spoiled everything.

'Hey, Jane, wake up!' Jane was nudged out of her thoughts by Buzz, who was passing her the plate of fortune cookies. 'Take one,' he said, 'and find out all about your future.' She took one and handed the plate to Stan. She should be able to eat a Chinese cookie. She had eaten them many times at birthday parties when she was a little girl.

Marcy broke open her cookie. 'Listen to this. I'm going to have a career,' she said. She read aloud from the slip of paper that had been inside her cookie. ' "You will be offered a high executive position with an attractive salary." '

Stan laughed. 'Marcy would rather have an attractive boss.'

'I hate you, Stan,' drawled Marcy, in a voice that told everyone she did not hate him at all. Jane and Julie exchanged a quick look. Marcy and her line!

'What does yours say, Julie?' Buzz asked.

Julie broke open her cookie. ' "Someone is speaking well of you," ' she read, and sighed. 'It's probably a dear old aunt.'

'I'll bet it's that boy you met at the mountains,' said Jane loyally. Julie had not met a boy when she went to the mountains with her family, but it would not hurt Buzz to think she had.

' "You will be called to fill a position of high honour and responsibility," ' read Greg from his slip.

'Congratulations!' exclaimed Buzz. 'I knew you'd get to be student-body president some day. Hey, listen to my fortune. Marcy isn't the only one who's going to be rich. "You will win prizes in contests testing your ability to answer questions." '

'It doesn't say you'll be rich,' scoffed Stan. 'It just says you'll win prizes. Probably a case of tooth paste or a year's supply of detergent.'

'And it doesn't say first prizes,' Marcy pointed out. 'Maybe you'll win a pie in the face because you don't know the answers.'

'You're jealous because you aren't quiz kids,' Buzz said smugly. 'What does yours say, Stan?'

Stan broke open his cookie and read, ' "Your place in the path of life is in the driver's seat." '

'Right in the front seat of the Doggie Diner truck,' said Marcy, and everyone laughed.

'I don't expect to make the Doggie Diner my career in the path of life,' Stan told Marcy. 'Jane, it's your turn.'

Hoping that her fortune would be a good omen, Jane snapped open her cookie and unfolded the slip of paper. ' "Prepare for a short journey",' she read.

'All the way back to Woodmont,' observed Marcy, and munched her cookie.

'How short can a journey get?' remarked Greg.

That's right thought Jane. Prepare for a short journey back to Woodmont and right out of Stan's life. I'll bet Marcy can hardly wait.

'Let's prepare for Jane's short journey by getting out of here,' said Stan. 'We still have time to go for a walk through Chinatown.'

When they left the restaurant, they found that fog had settled over the city and was swirling through the narrow streets. Foghorns were bleating and groaning down by the bay. Saddened by the sounds, Jane shivered in her light suit.

'We'll meet you at the truck in forty-five minutes,' said Stan to the other couples as he put his hand on Jane's elbow. 'Come on, Jane, let's go window-shopping.'

Should she apologize for not enjoying the Chinese dinner, Jane wondered, as she and Stan strolled up the street together. Too dispirited to say anything at all, she walked beside Stan past the Chinese shops toward the tourist end of Chinatown. Maybe tomorrow she would be able to think what to say, but tonight she was too heartsick to do anything but wander through the fog.

'Here we are,' Stan said, breaking their silence as he led Jane into a warm shop that smelled of incense. He seemed to be looking for something among the vases and bowls and embroidered slippers, but Jane had lost interest in everything but her own unhappiness. Stan selected a bamboo backscratcher from several stuck in a brass teapot and handed the proprietor some change.

'Here,' Stan said, offering the back-scratcher to Jane with a smile. 'A present for you.'

'For me?' exclaimed Jane in amazement, as she took the bamboo implement and stared at the little hand carved at the end of the long handle. 'A back-scratcher for me?'

'Yes, for you. Buying a back-scratcher in Chinatown is practically compulsory, didn't you know? All the tourists do it.'

Jane looked up at Stan and laughed, partly from amusement and partly because she was filled with a wonderful feeling of relief. Stan had bought her a back-scratcher! Maybe he wasn't disappointed in her after all.

'I think there may even be a law that says buying a

back-scratcher in Chinatown is compulsory,' Stan went on, and he and Jane laughed together.

They wandered out of the shop and on down the street through the swirling fog and now Jane was warmed by their laughter. In front of an ordinary American restaurant, the kind with a counter, a jukebox, and half a dozen booths, Stan turned and looked directly at Jane. 'You didn't have a good time at dinner, did you?' he asked.

Hot with embarrassment, Jane looked down at the sidewalk. She did not want to answer.

'Did you?' Stan persisted.

Jane looked up at him and shook her head. She had to be honest with Stan. 'It was just that it was all so strange,' she said. 'I never ate in a real Chinese restaurant before. It wasn't – quite what I expected.'

'I'm sorry,' Stan said contritely. 'I should have thought. I remember I felt the same way the first time I went there.'

Surprised and touched by his apology, Jane smiled at Stan. He didn't think she was a poor sport. He blamed himself for spoiling her evening, when all the time she had been worrying because she had spoiled his. 'I can't say I enjoyed it, but at the same time I'm not sorry we went there,' Jane told him. 'I guess you would call it an – an interesting experience.'

Stan no longer looked worried. 'I've felt that way about things myself,' he said, and glanced toward the restaurant. 'I'll bet you're hungry. How about a plain old American hamburger?'

Suddenly Jane was ravenous. 'I would adore a plain old American hamburger,' she said joyfully, and went into the restaurant with Stan.

They sat at the counter, and after Stan had ordered a

hamburger and a glass of milk for Jane, he swivelled his stool around so that he faced her. With a finger tip he touched a lock of her hair. 'You have little drops of fog clinging to your hair,' he told her.

'Do I?' Jane's hand flew to her fog-damp hair and she glanced at the mirror behind the counter.

'You know something?' said Stan.

'What?' asked Jane.

'You're different from most girls.'

'Am I?'

'Yes. You were so swell about having to go in the truck.'

'I was sort of surprised,' Jane admitted, 'but I didn't really mind.'

'Most girls would have made me feel I'd spoiled their evening, because riding to the city in a Doggie Diner truck was beneath their dignity or something. Or they would be like Marcy and make fun of it. But with you it didn't really matter that I couldn't get the car.'

Jane looked shyly down at the counter and ran her finger along the design in the handle of the back-scratcher – the precious back-scratcher, her present from Stan. 'No, it really didn't,' she whispered. She picked up the hamburger the waitress set before her and, as she bit hungrily into it, her eyes met Stan's in the mirror. Stan was smiling at her.

CHAPTER

6

'Love me on Monday, but don't love me one day. Love me on Tuesday ...' Jane sang in a throaty voice as she tossed her schoolbooks on to her bed. She pulled a comb through her hair and, smiling dreamily, paused to run a finger over the design on her back-scratcher, now tied to her mirror with a red ribbon. Then she kicked off her shoes and plopped herself cross-legged on the bed. English and French and math assignments could wait. Jane was knitting Stan a pair of Argyle socks for Christmas.

With awkward fingers she untangled the bobbins of green and yellow yarn and, after reading the directions twice to make sure, began to knit from a ball of grey wool. 'Love me on Tuesday, don't make it a blues day,' she hummed happily, as she thought back over the first week of school. It had been a wonderful week. All her daydreams had come true and, in the matter of locker assignments, had even been improved upon by the administration of Woodmont High. Stan's locker was almost directly across the hall from hers. This stroke of good luck was something not even Jane had dreamed of, and she marvelled at it several times a day when she saw Stan across the hall. Another piece of good fortune was that Stan's history class met in the room next to her French class. They even had the same lunch period and although Stan ate with a group of boys and Jane with several girls, they usually met on the lawn toward the end of the period and walked to their lockers together.

This was enough to establish Jane as Stan's girl in the eyes of Woodmont High, and because she was Stan's girl, Jane floated through the week in an aura of joy. She was no longer Jane Purdy, onlooker. She was Jane Purdy, Stan Crandall's girl. She belonged. The other students watched her walk down the hall beside Stan and thought, Jane and Stan. . . . And she was able to say, 'Stan and I . . .' Memories floated through Jane's mind. Stan holding the handle of the drinking fountain for her. Stan sitting beside her on the front steps of the school, the golden-brown hair on his arms glinting in the sunlight. The touch of his identification bracelet against her wrist as his arm brushed hers in the crowded hall. Stan's greenish eyes smiling down at her as he leaned against her locker, or waited for her outside her French room, or stood in the same line in the cafeteria. Oh, it had been a wonderful week.

Jane paused to untangle the bobbins that dangled from her knitting, and her eye fell on the first issue of the *Woodmontonian*, which had slipped out of her notebook when she tossed her books on to the bed. Listed in a box in the centre of the front page were the school social activities for the semester. Jane put down her knitting and picked up the paper. The list began with a tea to introduce the freshmen to the faculty (thank goodness, she was past *that* stage). Next was an informal dance to be held in the school gymnasium on Friday night, just one week away. This was followed by the junior-class steak bake and movie in Woodmont Park the first week in October, a show put

93

on by all the school clubs in November, and a Christmas formal in December.

An informal dance a week away. Jane read the story in the left-hand column of the paper, which told about the dance : music by Bob Starr and his All-Stars, a girl singer who had made a record that was tenth place on the Hit Parade, the members of the ticket committee and the decorating committee. Dreamily Jane went on with her knitting, unaware that she was working yellow wool into her pattern when she should have been using green. She saw herself circling the Woodmont High gym floor in Stan's arms and she would wear ... She did not know what she would wear, but she was sure of one thing. She had enough baby-sitting money to buy a pair of shoes with real high heels, beautiful airy shoes – heels, thin soles, and wisps of leather to hold them on her feet, shoes so light she would scarcely know she was wearing them as she whirled in Stan's arms.

Of course, Stan had not actually asked her to go to the dance yet. ... Jane dismissed this detail from her mind. When a boy sees a girl every day and takes her to dinner in the city and buys her a back-scratcher and notices the fog on her hair, naturally he asks her to go to the first school dance. He just hadn't got around to it yet. And this time maybe he could take the family car.

Just before dinner on Saturday the telephone rang. '*Arf-arf!*' barked Mr Purdy. Since the night Jane had ridden to the city in the Doggie Diner truck, he had taken to barking every time the telephone or doorbell rang.

'Pop! Really!' protested Jane good-naturedly, as she went hopefully to the telephone. Honestly, the things that amused her father!

It was not Stan but Julie who was calling. 'Jane, guess what!' Julie was in an obvious state of excitement. 'Buzz asked me to go to the dance next Friday!'

'Julie! Did he really? How perfectly wonderful!' Jane was happy for her, not only because Julie was her best friend but because now she and Stan could trade dances with Buzz and Julie and perhaps see less of Marcy and whatever boy she chose to go with. Somehow, Jane did not like to think of Stan's dancing with Marcy.

'Stan has asked you to go, hasn't he?' Julie wanted to know.

'Not exactly,' said Jane cautiously. 'Not yet, but I'm seeing him tonight. We're going to the movies.'

'And Jane,' Julie went on, too engrossed in her own anticipation to notice Jane's hesitation, 'Buzz's dad says he can take the car that night!'

'What wonderful luck!' agreed Jane.

'If Stan can't get his car maybe we could double-date,' Julie suggested.

'That would be fun,' answered Jane, 'but I hope he can get the car.'

That evening on the way to the movies and afterwards at Nibley's and on the walk home, Jane waited for Stan to mention the dance. He was unusually talkative and told her about the different dogs on his route – the pair of Dalmatians that waited for him and the boxer that chased the truck so far he often had to give the dog a ride home – but he did not mention the dance. Oh, well, thought Jane, that's how men are. He's probably taking it for granted. She found it very pleasant to be taken for granted by Stan.

By Monday morning it was impossible for any student

to ignore the fact that Woodmont High was having a dance on Friday night. Posters in the shape of autumn leaves and footballs appeared on every bulletin board, banners were hung across the halls, and a reminder to get your tickets now, one dollar per couple, was printed in the daily bulletin. When Stan walked across the hall to Jane's locker to say hello, she said, 'The dance committee must have put in a lot of hard work over the weekend to get all those posters up.'

'It sure did,' agreed Stan. 'Well, so long. I've got to pick up a reserved book at the libe before class.'

Jane stood with her hand on her locker door, looking uncertainly after Stan as he made his way through the crowd in the direction of the library. It almost seemed as if he had been in a hurry to get away from her when she mentioned the dance. Naturally he was in a hurry, she told herself. He didn't have time to stand around talking when he had to go to the library, check out a book, and walk downstairs again before first period. Still . . .

'What are you looking so wistful about?' asked Liz Galpin, who had been assigned to share the locker with Jane. Liz was also a member of Manuscript. She submitted pieces entitled 'Life and Death : a Dialogue' or simply 'Hokku'. A hokku was a Japanese poem that had seventeen syllables. When Jane tried to write a hokku it always turned out to have sixteen or twenty syllables, never seventeen.

'Was I looking wistful?' Jane answered lightly. I didn't know it showed, she thought. There was something about Liz, with her dark-rimmed glasses and her hair chopped off any old way, as if it didn't matter how she looked, that made Jane feel fluffy and not very bright.

'You looked positively lovelorn,' said Liz as she stowed a couple of thin books, poetry probably, in their locker.

'It must be something I ate,' answered Jane, trying to look bored like Marcy. She closed the locker, snapped shut the combination lock, and was about to go to her first-period study hall when she saw George, the old family friend, coming purposefully toward her.

'Hi,' she said, wondering why he was taking the trouble to cross the crowded hall to speak to her.

'Hello, Jane,' he said. 'How about going to the dance with me Friday night?' He spoke rapidly, as if he were anxious to get the words out of the way.

Jane could feel the blood rush to her face. She had been so engrossed in Stan that it had never occurred to her anyone else might ask her to go to the dance. By this time she thought it was obvious to everyone at Woodmont High that she was Stan's girl. But apparently it was not obvious to George, who was probably so busy with his rock collection and his chemistry experiments that he hadn't noticed. That was George for you – oblivious, buried in science, with that lock of hair sticking up as usual.

What an awful situation! How perfectly awful! Jane ran one finger down the louvres on her locker and stared at the floor while she tried to think what to say that would not hurt George's feelings, yet would leave her free to go to the dance with Stan. She had to choose her words with care. Going to the dance with George was out of the question. Loping around the gym trying to appear two inches shorter than she was, when she had dreamed of whirling in Stan's arms in her first high heels! It was impossible.

If she said she already had a date with Stan she wouldn't be telling the truth and George might know it.

If she said she was busy Friday evening and then George took another girl to the dance and she turned up with Stan – well, that wouldn't do either. But she couldn't just stand there. She had to say something. 'I – I'm sorry, George,' she said at last. 'I already have a date for Friday night.' And she told herself she did – almost.

'Well, O.K. Some other time maybe.' George's face was as flushed with embarrassment as Jane's.

He knows, thought Jane miserably. George had guessed that she didn't want to go with him and that she didn't really have a date. He might be oblivious about a lot of things, but he wasn't stupid.

They stood facing one another, Jane ashamed to have hurt George's feelings and George embarrassed to have his feelings hurt, uncertain of what to say next, until the sound of the first bell clanging through the hall rescued them.

'See you around,' muttered George, and disappeared into the stream of students moving toward their clasrooms.

Well, I don't care, thought Jane defiantly. I do have a date – sort of. And anyway, she had always suspected George's mother made him take her out, because she was an old friend of the family ; his mother probably told him she was a sweet, sensible girl. But Jane did care. Because she had hurt the feelings of someone she liked, she felt uneasy and uncomfortable all the rest of the day. On the way home from school she walked past the shoe store without stopping to search the windows for the dancing shoes she dreamed about – the delicate shoes with heels, soles, and mere wisps of leather to hold them to her feet. Darn Stan anyway.

By Tuesday morning Jane was cheerful again. This

was the day Stan would mention the dance. He had just forgotten – men were so absent-minded about such things – and he had been carrying the tickets in his wallet all the time.

As usual he crossed the hall to her locker and said, 'Hi, Jane.'

'Hi,' she said, and waited.

'Old Hargrave is really piling it on in maths,' he said. 'I thought I was going to be up all night on his assignment.'

Plainly Stan was not thinking about the dance and yet Jane did not see how he could forget it, when the whole school was plastered with banners and posters and cardboard autumn leaves.

Later in the morning a girl in Jane's algebra class remarked wistfully, 'I suppose you're going to the dance with Stan.'

Jane smiled and said nothing. A smile could mean anything.

'Of course you're going to the dance with Stan,' said another girl, in the cafeteria during lunch period.

'Could be,' said Jane. 'I hope they're serving lemon pie today.'

'You're sure lucky,' answered the girl. 'I wish a new boy would turn up for me.'

Jane realized the situation was getting complicated. She could not honestly say she was going to the dance with Stan, and neither could she say she was not going with him. Her pride would not let her admit to anyone that she had not been asked. It would be all over school in half an hour. Everyone would talk and wonder. The boys would think she wasn't any fun on a date and the girls would start inviting Stan to parties and asking him to help them with their maths. And what would she be doing? Drinking cokes with the girls on Saturday nights.

It was while she was playing volley ball during her gym class that Jane made up her mind that she could not stand this uncertainty any longer. A few minutes before, while she was changing into her shirt and shorts in the locker room, two girls had asked her what she was going to wear Friday night. Waiting her turn to serve, Jane decided that when Stan walked down the hall with her between sixth and seventh periods she would bring up the dance once more and find out for certain whether she had a date or not. She was sure she did – well, pretty sure – but she wanted to hear Stan say so himself. Satisfied that she had at least made a decision, Jane gave the volley ball a vicious whack that sent it out of bounds.

That afternoon when Stan met Jane outside her French class she said gaily, '*Bonjour.*'

Stan grinned at her. '*Onjourbay*,' he answered. 'French pig Latin. How's that for class?'

Jane laughed, but her thoughts were fixed on bringing up the subject of the dance. Her mouth was dry, and all the gay, casual remarks she had composed during her French class had slipped away from her. If this continued much longer she was sure to flunk everything. Only a few minutes ago she had not bothered to look up *colère* in the vocabulary and had translated '*Il était emporté par sa colère*' as 'He was dragged away by his collar,' when it should have been 'He was carried away by his anger.' The laughter of the class still rang in her ears.

Silently the two made their way through the stream of students toward Jane's English classroom. I've got to say something, Jane thought wildly. Something light, something casual, something that would let her know for sure and yet not reveal to Stan how important this was to her.

When they reached the door of Room 214, Jane turned to Stan. This was the moment. Somehow, words came out of her mouth, and they were not at all the words she had meant to speak. 'George asked me to go to the dance Friday, but I said I already had a date,' she blurted out.

An expression – could it be relief? – crossed Stan's face. 'Hey, that's swell!' Stan was enthusiastic about something; just what, Jane was not sure. She stared at him, shocked by his reaction.

'If you have a date we can trade dances,' Stan went on.

'But I don't,' Jane cried out in spite of herself. 'I thought –'

The bell clanging through the hall stopped Jane from saying any more, but she could not help giving Stan one stricken look. His expression changed from enthusiasm to bewilderment, embarrassment, and, worst of all – how could she bear it? – pity. Silently Jane fled into Room 214, and Miss Locke, her English teacher, closed the door behind her.

The efforts of Miss Locke to teach clear thinking in English composition were wasted on Jane during the next hour. Squinting modifiers, dangling participles – who cared? All she could think about was herself and Stan. Now it was all so painfully clear. Now, when it was too late to undo what she had done. Stan had asked another girl (What girl? Who could she be?) to go to the dance, when she had assumed he would ask her. And she had let him know she expected him to ask her, and now he felt sorry for her. Never in her life had Jane felt so hurt, so humiliated.

Of course Stan had a right to ask anyone he pleased to the dance. But she had thought . . . she had wanted . . . she had been so sure. He was everything she liked in a boy. Oh, how could Miss Locke stand there and go on about squinting modifiers? How could she care? The irony of it all, having to sit through Miss Locke's lesson in clear thinking after she had been so dumb! Stan was so nice to be with and she had been so sure . . . But she had no right to be sure. She knew that now. If only she had known it before she spoke to Stan. Stan, who now felt sorry for her, poor little Jane Purdy, the girl who got her hopes up, just because he had had a few dates with her and had bought her a back-scratcher. A back-scratcher! How silly it seemed now. How could she have taken it so seriously? A back-scratcher!

But even though Stan had asked some other girl to go to the dance, even though he felt sorry for her, Jane could not dislike Stan. It wasn't his fault she was so stupid. She could never, never face him again, but she still liked him. She would avoid him in the hall, keep her books in Julie's locker, forget him if she could. A few dates, and one wonderful week at school, and now she was no longer Jane Purdy, Stan's girl, a girl who belonged. She was plain Jane Purdy, a nice girl but nobody special. It was all over.

Now if she were the kind of girl Marcy was, nothing like this would ever happen. If she were like Marcy, Stan would want to take her to the dance and would have asked her for a date way ahead to be sure no other boy would ask her first. And then the thought came to Jane that Stan might be taking Marcy to the dance. She remembered the way they had talked together in the Chinese restaurant. But no, he couldn't be taking Marcy. She would have heard about it before now – unless everyone was trying to keep it from her so her feelings wouldn't be hurt.

Jane stared blankly at the blackboard while Miss Locke wrote with squeaking chalk, 'Some members of the class I know are not paying attention.' Miss Locke always liked to relate her examples to the experience of her students. Several girls laughed politely.

'Jane,' said Miss Locke, pointing to the sentence with the chalk, 'can you tell us what is wrong with this sentence?'

Jane forced her eyes to focus on the blackboard. The words were meaningless. 'I'm sorry, Miss Locke,' she said. 'I guess I wasn't paying attention.' This brought a loud laugh from several boys in the back of the room and a titter from the rest of the class.

'Elizabeth, will you tell Jane what is wrong with the sentence?' asked Miss Locke.

' "I know" squints,' answered Liz promptly. 'The sentence should read, "I know some members of the class are not paying attention" or "Some members of the class are not paying attention, I know." '

Jane tried to look as if she were absorbing this bit of knowledge, but all the time she was thinking desperately, Will I be so dumb about boys when I am sixteen? Will I still be so dumb?

CHAPTER

7

WHEN the bell finally brought to a close the period that she should have devoted to clear thinking in English composition, Jane knew that she could not face Stan. She dawdled over her books at her desk and then, with her back turned toward the door, paused by the blackboard to ask Miss Locke some hastily composed questions about the next day's assignment. On Tuesday Stan had to leave school in a hurry to start his Doggie Diner route. When five minutes had clicked by on the electric clock, she was sure that Stan was gone and that she was safe.

Abruptly Jane thanked Miss Locke and fled down the hall to Julie's locker. 'Julie, something awful has happened. I'll tell you on the way home. May I keep my books in your locker?' The whispered words came out in a rush.

Julie looked at her in surprise. 'Why, sure. You can use my locker any time. You know the combination.' She lowered her voice to a whisper. 'What happened?'

'I can't tell you here,' said Jane. 'Julie, do me a favour. Go to my locker and get out all my books.'

'All right. If you want me to.' Julie looked mystified, but she did as Jane asked. Jane selected the books she needed for her homework, stored the rest in Julie's locker, and hurried out of the building with her friend.

'Quick, tell me,' begged Julie. 'I can't stand the suspense any longer.'

Miserably Jane poured out the story.

Julie was silent while she considered the implications of Jane's problem. 'How ghastly!' she said at last. 'How perfectly ghastly!'

'Yes,' agreed Jane unhappily. 'I don't know what to do. At least I didn't come right out and tell anybody he was taking me to the dance.'

'I wonder who he is taking,' mused Julie.

'I don't know,' said Jane. 'The way things get around school you'd think I'd have heard by now. And what I can't understand is why he's taking someone else. We'd been getting along so well and having such fun together. And he took me to the city and – and everything.' Her voice trailed off as she remembered the way Stan had looked at her when he ordered the hamburger for her in Chinatown.

'Maybe he has to take the boss's daughter, or something,' suggested Julie.

'No, that isn't it,' said Jane gloomily. 'His cousin owns the Doggie Diner and if he has a daughter she's probably about two years old.'

'Maybe he's taking his sister.' This was far-fetched, but Julie was trying to be comforting.

'No, one is too old and the other is too young. Anyway, Stan isn't the type to take his sister to a dance.'

The two girls walked in silence, Jane lost in humiliation and Julie quiet out of sympathy for her friend. When they reached Julie's house, Julie said, 'Come on in for a coke. Maybe we can think of something.'

'No, thanks. Not today,' answered Jane, and hesitated. 'Julie, do you think ... Stan could be taking Marcy?'

Julie looked serious. 'I don't know. I hadn't thought of

that, but it's a possibility. She talked to him a lot that night in Chinatown.'

'Do you suppose you could sort of ask around and find out who she's going with?' This was a favour Jane did not like to ask, even from Julie, but she felt she had to find out. 'But don't let anybody know I want to know,' she cautioned.

'Sure, Jane, I'll try to find out and let you know. And say, I just had an idea. Buzz might know somebody who needs a date,' said Julie. 'Maybe he could arrange something for you.'

'No, it wouldn't be the same,' said Jane. She could not let it get around school that Buzz was trying to dig up a date for poor little Jane Purdy, the girl Stan Crandall used to go with. Maybe she wasn't one of *the* crowd, but she still wasn't the kind of girl who had to have dates dug up for her. Besides, if she couldn't go to the dance with Stan, she didn't want to go with anyone.

'No, I suppose it wouldn't be the same,' agreed Julie.

Feeling more lonely than ever, Jane hurried home to the privacy of her own room. She threw her books on the bed, untied the ribbon that held her back-scratcher to the edge of her mirror, and flung the piece of carved wood into her wastebasket. She stared at it lying among the lipstick-smeared Kleenex and, after a moment of hesitation, took it out again and hid it at the back of a drawer under a pile of sweaters. Then she sat down on her bed and yanked the needles out of the Argyle sock she had been knitting. It was not very good knitting, anyway. The sock was grubby from being ravelled and reknit so many times to correct mistakes and, no matter how often Jane read the directions, the yellow stripes that ran across the green diamonds refused to go straight. Jane found a gloomy satisfaction in jerking out the stitches. There, she thought, when the last stitch was unravelled. There goes Stan out of my life. It was all over and done with, and all there was for her to do was to forget him.

But the next day Jane found it was not easy to forget someone she had to work so hard to avoid. She had to get to her classes early and by devious instead of direct routes to keep from running into Stan. At noon she did not go to the cafeteria but sat instead on the steps of the gym and nibbled at a sandwich and an apple from home. She found, too, that she not only had to avoid Stan, but everyone else as well. She could not face the questions the other girls might ask her about the dance or their speculations when they heard she had not been asked by Stan. It was a lonely week. And as the week wore on, the silence of the Purdy telephone told her that Stan was avoiding her too. In a miserable sort of way she was glad. She never wanted to see him or talk to him again. Never. Especially if he was taking Marcy to the dance.

On Friday evening, while Jane was picking at her dinner, the telephone rang.

'*Arf-arf!*' barked Mr Purdy.

'Pop!' pleaded Jane in real anguish as she left the table. Out of the corner of her eye she saw her mother frown ever so slightly and shake her head at her father. Mr Purdy looked surprised and then indicated by his expression that he understood something was wrong.

So Mom has guessed, thought Jane, as she picked up the receiver. Now her family and her school and probably all of Woodmont knew that something was wrong between her and Stan. As she had expected, the call was from Julie.

'Did you find out?' Jane asked in a dull voice.

'Yes, finally,' answered Julie. 'I had a hard time, because I didn't like to come right out and ask anybody. You know. So I sort of had to go around with my ear to the ground. And then I happened to be walking past the drugstore and I heard a girl say something about Marcy and I slowed down –'

'Julie, just tell me. Is Stan taking Marcy?' Jane begged.

'No,' said Julie. 'Marcy is going with that cute boy in the school-bus, the one that broke up with that girl who wears the tight skirts –'

'I know the one,' said Jane. So it wasn't Marcy. That was something.

'That was only half of what I called about,' Julie continued. 'Mrs Lashbrook called for a sitter for Nadine this evening. It's awfully short notice, but I wondered if you would want the job.'

Since I'm not doing anything else – Jane finished the sentence silently. Julie might as well have said it out loud. 'I guess so,' she said halfheartedly. Nadine, an eleven-year-old bookworm, was no trouble to sit with. 'What time?'

'Mr Lashbrook will pick you up at seven,' Julie told her.

'O.K.,' said Jane. She hesitated before adding, 'Have a good time tonight, Julie. And Julie, call me in the morning and tell me about . . . everything.'

'Sure,' agreed Julie, and the sympathy in her voice was genuine. 'I'll call you the first thing and . . . let you know.'

Numb with misery, Jane assembled a stack of textbooks

to take to the Lashbrooks' for the evening. Their house was quiet, Nadine would be buried in a book, and this would be a good chance to do a lot of studying and try to make up for the poor grades she had earned so far in the semester. She would put Stan and dates out of her mind and devote her time to her studies. No more C's or even B's for her. From now on she would get straight A's. She would be known throughout Woodmont High as Jane Purdy, the brain. Her name would be engraved on the silver scholarship cup in the trophy case at school. She would write intellectual essays for Manuscript like Liz Galpin, instead of childish articles entitled 'Springtime in Yosemite National Park' or 'My Experiences as a Baby-Sitter.' Or sonnets might be better. If a new boy came to Woodmont High he would wonder who this attractive Jane Purdy was who made such wonderful grades. And everyone would say, That is Jane, our top student, straight A plusses, who has such a brilliant career ahead of her that she can't waste her time on boys. When she finished high school she would have a selection of scholarships to choose from. She would go to one of those Eastern women's colleges. . . .

Jane recalled her English II teacher, who once said sarcastically, when Jane had failed to look up *albeit* in the dictionary during the study of *As You Like It*, 'Jane Purdy, have you no intellectual curiosity?' Well, she may not have had any intellectual curiosity in English II, but she did now.

By the time Jane arrived at the Lashbrooks' she was filled with a comforting feeling of martyrdom. The Lashbrooks were among her favourite baby-sitting customers. They always came home before midnight, they always had the right change to pay her, and they lived in a gracious old redwood house set in a grove of redwood trees in the hills. The wood-panelled living-room, fragrant with eucalyptus wood burning in the stone fireplace, was inviting, and Jane looked around the room with pleasure. She liked the worn Oriental rugs, the comfortable chairs slip-covered in faded linen, the mellow furniture waxed until it glowed and flickered in reflected light from the fire. Tonight there was a brass bowl of apples on the coffee table, and the open curtains framed a view through the redwood trees of Woodmont below and the bay and the city in the distance.

Nadine, a pale, spindling child, was curled up in a chair with a book. 'Hello, Jane,' she said, barely lifting her eyes from *The Pinto Stallion Revolts Again* long enough to peer at her sitter through her glasses. From time to time she sniffed. Nadine was allergic to cats and house dust, and although the Lashbrooks did not keep a cat, no one had ever figured out what to do about house dust.

'We should be home by eleven. The number is beside the telephone in case you want us,' said Mrs Lashbrook. Noticing Jane's pile of books, she added, 'You may use Mr Lashbrook's desk if you wish,' and cleared a pile of papers out of the way. 'Good night, girls. Go to bed at nine, won't you, Nadine?'

'Yes,' said Nadine, turning a page and reading avidly.

Jane sat down at the big desk that faced the room and the view, and briskly prepared to study. She opened her notebook, got out several sheets of paper, and pulled her English book out of the stack of texts. Brilliant students did not waste time. Then she read the assignment. 'Rewrite a scene from *Julius Caesar* in modern English.'

Feeling pleasantly intellectual to be spending part of her evening with Shakespeare, Jane flipped through the book until she found the play.

Nadine gave a loud sniff, rose from her chair, and without raising her eyes from her book, walked across the room, took an apple from the bowl on the coffee table, returned to her chair, and curled up again.

You'd think she'd trip over something, thought Jane, and turned to Shakespeare. Nadine gave a loud sniff and crunched into the apple.

Jane read, 'Act One. Scene One. Rome. A street. Enter Flavius, Marullus, and certain Commoners.' There didn't seem to be anything to change about that. It was modern enough. She read on. '*Flavius:* Hence! home, you idle creatures, get you home! Is this a holiday?' Jane considered this. Because she was full of intellectual curiosity this evening, she consulted the cast of characters to see who this Flavius was. He was a tribune. Some sort of old Roman army officer, she thought, although today a tribune sounded more like a newspaper.

Nadine sniffed again, chewed noisily, and stopped abruptly.

Jane waited. Well, go on and chew, she thought. Finish the bite. Nadine turned a page and, except for the snapping of the fire, the room was silent. Suddenly she began to chew vigorously once more.

She must have come to an exciting part of the story, Jane thought. Now to get back to Shakespeare. 'Hence! home, you idle creatures' in modern English? Jane stared out the window at the lights on the bridges, strung like two golden necklaces across the bay. After a moment's thought she wrote down, '*Flavius:* Scram!' She looked critically at her work. This was not right. This did not fit into the picture of herself as a brilliant student. Miss Locke had said modern English, not slang.

Nadine had eaten the skin off the apple and was now gnawing her way around the core in a series of rapid nibbles without pausing to take the apple away from her mouth. Nibble, nibble, nibble, sniff. Silence.

Well, go on, thought Jane, distracted from *Julius Caesar*. Go on, chew it. Nadine prolonged the silence and suddenly began to eat again. Nibble, nibble, nibble, sniff. Jane relaxed. She crossed out 'Scram' and wrote down, '*Flavius:* Go home.' Somehow that was not the effect she wanted to achieve, either. This old Tribune Flavius should be more forceful. He shouldn't sound as if he were ordering a dog out of a begonia bed. No, this was not the sort of thing a brilliant student would write. However, if Flavius could sort of orate instead of just yelling, 'Go home,' it might sound more intellectual. Jane wondered if Miss Locke would object to the addition of directions. '*Flavius* (orating): Go home.' Most likely Miss Locke would not approve. She would want her students to think of a forceful phrase that would convey the meaning without directions. That was Miss Locke for you.

The nibbles grew smaller and faster as Nadine turned the apple core in her fingers. She'll be eating the whole thing, seeds and all, if she doesn't look at it once in a while, thought Jane, as she looked up from *Julius Caesar*. Through the window she noticed soft fingers of fog slipping across the bay. She found herself thinking of Stan and the night in the city when he had touched her fog-damp hair and smiled at her. And now he was dancing with another girl, someone he liked better than Jane. Who could she be, Jane wondered. Someone from one of his classes, or a girl who lived near him? And would he touch her hair and smile down at her, too? But she must not think about it. Resolutely Jane turned back to her work and studied the next phrase, 'you idle creatures'. Now what did that mean? Were these men lazy or were they unemployed?

Somewhere in the house a clock struck nine. Nadine stood up and tossed her apple core into the fireplace. 'Good night,' she said and, still reading, walked out of the room.

'Good night, Nadine,' answered Jane, marvelling that the girl did not bump into the furniture.

The eucalyptus log in the fireplace burned through and sank into a pile of coals. A chill and a silence, magnified by the hum of the refrigerator in the kitchen, settled over the house. This was the lonely hour of baby-sitting, when the house was still and the minutes began to drag. Two more hours. Jane sat staring at the first scene of *Julius Caesar* until the sound of the furnace turning itself on made her start. Quietly she closed her book. She did not want to be a brilliant student. She did not want to be intellectually curious. She wanted to be Stan's girl, dancing with him in the gymnasium of Woodmont High.

Jane walked to the window and stood looking out over the lights of the town at the fog that billowed over the bay, blotting out the bridges and the city. The sound of a car driving up the road only made the house seem lonelier. In the distance the foghorns had begun their melancholy chorus. *Yoo-hoo* boomed a horn far away. *Yoo-hoo. Come back* moaned another near the bridge. *Come back*.

Jane pressed her forehead against the cool glass. The

dance had started and Stan was dancing with the other girl, the girl he had asked because he did not want to take Jane. And when the girl singer who had made the record that was tenth place on the Hit Parade began to sing, everyone would stop dancing and gather round the bandstand. Stan and the girl would stand close together and Stan would put his arm around the girl. . . .

Tomorrow Jane would know who the girl was. Julie would tell her, but she might never know why Stan had invited the girl to go to the dance. The humiliation that Jane had felt turned to something else – grief perhaps, or regret. Regret that she had not known how to act with a boy, regret that she had not been wiser. Perhaps next year when she was sixteen ...

The creeping fingers of fog began to blot out the lights of Woodmont below. *Come back, come back* moaned the foghorn, only to be mocked in the distance. *Yoo-hoo, yoo-hoo.*

Ten years from now I'll look back on this night and laugh, Jane thought. But she knew in her heart it was not true. In ten years she might look back, but she would not laugh, not even then. This night was too painful to laugh about ever. Jane knew that. Slowly two tears brimmed her eyes and slid down her cheeks.

Come back, pleaded one foghorn. *Yoo-hoo*, mocked the other.

CHAPTER

8

SATURDAY morning, soon after breakfast, Julie phoned.

'Hi,' said Jane, as cheerfully as she could. 'Did you have a good time last night?'

'Wonderful,' answered Julie. 'The music was good and Buzz is a smooth dancer, although I do wish he was a little bit taller.'

'I'm glad you had a good time,' said Jane. There was a moment of silence. Both girls hesitated to bring up the real reason for this telephone call, Jane because she dreaded finding out the name of the other girl, and Julie because she knew the whole incident was distressing to her friend.

Jane was first to break the silence. 'Who was she?' she asked bluntly.

'A girl from the city.'

'Oh.' Jane had never considered the possibility of Stan's having a girl in the city.

'She was sort of an old family friend,' Julie went on. 'Anyway, she came over to Woodmont with Stan's dad after work and had dinner with his family before the dance.'

Jane felt a little better. She would not have to face Stan's other girl at school. Maybe Stan's father had made him take her to the dance because she was an old family friend. Maybe the girl was long and lanky and stepped all over Stan's shoes. Maybe she even had pimples.

'Stan called her Bitsy,' said Julie.

'Bitsy?' Jane thought she had misunderstood. 'Don't you mean Betsy?'

'No. Bitsy. Everybody calls her Bitsy, because she is such a little bitsy thing.'

Jane detected more than a trace of cattiness in Julie's voice as her friend continued. 'You know the type. She had to wear real high heels, because she is so little. The type that makes the other girls feel big and awkward. Especially me. She made me feel all wool and a yard wide as if I should be running around with a hockey stick instead of dancing.'

'What did she look like?' Jane persisted. She had to know all the details, no matter how disturbing they might be. And so far they were very disturbing indeed.

A gusty sigh from Julie came over the telephone. 'Well . . . I hate to say it, but she was perfectly darling.'

That, thought Jane, is that. Even if she was an old family friend, Stan's father did not make him take her to the dance. If she was perfectly darling, Stan took her because he wanted to. Stan's darling little Bitsy.

Julie sighed again. 'She was real smooth and she had one of those sleek new haircuts.' Jane resolved to stop snipping off her own hair with the manicure scissors. 'And most of the girls were wearing full skirts,' said Julie, 'but not Bitsy. She wore a dress with a straight skirt. You know, simple and sort of elegant, like you see in the shop windows in the city.'

'Yes, I know,' agreed Jane. 'The kind that even if we had the money our mothers would say we couldn't buy because they were too sophisticated for us.'

'Exactly.'

'And I suppose she has a terrible time finding anything to wear in her size, because she is so little.' Jane found a certain relish in being catty herself.

'How did you guess?' Julie sounded surprised. 'That's exactly what she said when we were putting on fresh lipstick during intermission.'

Jane had to know everything. 'Was she nice?'

'Yes, she really was,' said Julie regretfully. 'She was friendly with everyone. Everybody liked her and the fellows really went for her.'

'Oh.' Jane felt this was the end. She did not have a chance with a smooth girl – a little bitsy smooth girl – from the city. A girl who was not only smooth, but a girl everyone liked. Probably the only reason Stan had taken Jane out at all was that she was handy. Good old Jane, always available for a date when Bitsy wasn't around. She brought herself up sharply. What was she thinking about anyway? This was not the end. The end had come that day outside her English class over a week ago, when she had put Stan out of her life forever.

'Jane, are you still there?' Julie asked.

'Yes. I was just thinking,' answered Jane. 'I suppose you traded dances?'

'Yes, and Stan is a wonderful dancer, in case that's what you're wondering.'

'Yes, I was wondering,' Jane admitted.

At that moment the doorbell rang.

'I've got to hang up,' said Jane hastily. 'There's somebody at the door and Mom's downtown.'

'Probably the Fuller brush man,' said Julie. ' 'Bye.'

Tucking in her shirt-tail with one hand, Jane opened the front door. Stan was standing on the front porch.

An electric feeling flashed through Jane, the same sensation she had felt the first time she had picked up the telephone and found that Stan, the strange boy who delivered horse meat, was on the line. She stood staring at him, and although she was unable to think of anything to say, she was aware that he was wearing a fresh white T-shirt and sharply creased sun tans and that his identification bracelet was still on his wrist. At least he didn't give his bracelet to Bitsy, thought Jane; not that it means anything to me.

'Hello, Jane,' said Stan, without smiling. 'I tried to call you this morning, but your line was busy.'

Jane felt her cheeks begin to burn, as all the hurt and humiliation of the last two weeks came back to her. And after the description of smooth little Bitsy she had heard from Julie, she felt awkward and untidy in her jeans and plaid shirt with her hair carelessly combed. 'Hello, Stan,' she managed to say, brushing aside a feeling of annoyance that a girl she had not even met could make her feel this way.

'Could you come for a ride with me?' Stan asked. 'I – I want to show you something.'

Jane tried to collect her thoughts. Stan needn't think he could treat her the way he did and then come around any old time and expect her to go out with him on a moment's notice. She wasn't going to be good old handy Jane Purdy. He needn't think he could take her for granted. She forgot that only the week before she had found it pleasant to be taken for granted by Stan. 'I'm sorry,' she said coolly. 'I have a baby-sitting engagement at eleven.'

Stan looked at his watch. 'It's only ten-fifteen. Come

for a ride and I'll drop you off. Please, Jane. I – I've got to talk to you.'

Of course I won't go, thought Jane. Then she wavered. For a moment she was undecided, but only for a moment. Curiosity won out. She had to find out what Stan wanted to show her and what he had to talk about. She would ride with him this once, but never again. She would be cool and aloof the whole time. Not that she would let him know her feelings were hurt. Nothing like that. Just . . . well, cool and aloof. 'All right,' she said in a polite, impersonal tone. 'Just a minute.'

Jane scribbled a note for her mother and jerked a comb through her hair. She did not bother to change her clothes, because she had found that jeans were practical to wear when sitting with little children. What difference did it make what she had on? Stan liked girls with sleek hair-cuts, who wore sophisticated clothes. Besides, it was all over between them and had been for over a week.

'Where's the truck?' Jane asked, as she and Stan started down the steps. The only car in sight was a blue coupé with the top down, which was parked in front of the house next door.

'We're not going in the truck,' said Stan. 'We're going in my car.'

'Your car!' Jane was so surprised she could not believe Stan meant what he said. He must be joking.

'That's right. My car. There it is,' said Stan proudly, pointing to the blue coupé. 'I wanted to surprise you.'

'Why, Stan!' Jane, forgetting to be cool and aloof, was astonished and delighted all at the same time. 'You mean it's your very own?'

'It sure is. I bought it with my Doggie Diner money and the money I saved from the paper route I had in the city.' Then he added apologetically, 'Of course, it isn't exactly new, and my cousin and I had to do a lot of work on it to get it to go, but it works all right now. And I have to leave the top down, because it's sort of ragged, but I hope to get a new top before the rainy season.'

'Why, Stan, how marvellous! How perfectly marvellous!' Jane stood admiring the car, and the thought flashed through her mind that now Stan would no longer have to hide his bicycle in the firethorn bushes. The car was a model-A Ford and, in the strictest definition of the word, a convertible. That is, it had a folding top. Or, to be more accurate, what was left of the top folded. The seat was neatly covered with an army blanket and the trim, which had very few dents, was polished until it twinkled in the sunlight. The fresh blue paint, which Jane felt was in quiet good taste and which had only a few streaks, gleamed. There was not a speck of dust on the car anywhere.

'Like it?' asked Stan.

'It's perfect,' said Jane, and meant it. The car was neither a jalopy nor a hot rod. It looked plain and serviceable, exactly right for riding around Woodmont.

'I knew you'd like it,' said Stan. 'Some girls might think it was old and funny, but I knew you wouldn't.'

'I think it's neat-looking,' commented Jane.

'So do I.' Stan held the door open for Jane. 'Hop in and let's go for a ride.'

Jane stepped on to the high running board and sat down on the army blanket. It seemed strange to be sitting up so high, and she found it much pleasanter than sitting in a modern car. The view was better. The car started easily. Jane shifted her position on the seat, because she was sitting on a broken spring, and rode in silent admiration. Somehow, Woodmont looked different when seen from a boy's own car. The air seemed clearer and the trees stood out more sharply against the sky line. A wisp of hair blew across her eyes, and Jane brushed it away with the same gesture Marcy used when she rode in Greg's father's convertible. This must be the way Marcy felt.

'I – I wanted you to be the first girl to ride in it,' Stan said.

'Did you really? Oh, Stan!' They drove past a girl who had been in Jane's math class and who was now walking toward the library with an armload of books.

'Hello there,' called Jane. Poor girl, going to the library on such a beautiful morning!

'Hi,' the girl answered, and looked wistfully at Stan and his car.

They drove into Woodmont Park, where Stan stopped under some bay trees by the stream. 'I didn't use my car last night, because I wanted you to be the first to ride in it,' he said, turning to Jane. 'I took Dad's car instead.'

Last night. The humiliation Jane had felt for the past week came rushing back. She could not look at Stan. 'I hope you had a good time,' she said stiffly, picking up a dry bay leaf that had drifted on to the seat between them, and twirling it around in her fingers.

'I guess I should have explained it all to you ahead of time,' said Stan miserably.

'You don't have to explain anything to me.' This time Jane was cool and aloof. She looked away from Stan and crumpled the bay leaf to release its fragrance. 'If you wanted to take another girl, there was no reason why you shouldn't.'

'But I didn't want to,' said Stan.

Oh, Stan, thought Jane, please don't try to make me believe your family made you take Bitsy because she is an old family friend.

'I mean, I didn't want to take her after I met you,' Stan went on. 'I used to take Bitsy out once in a while when I lived in the city. Her folks are friends of my folks and I sort of liked her. Anyway, just before we moved over here I told her I would have her over for the first school dance. I know it was a dumb thing to do, but after I had done it I couldn't very well break the date, especially since Mom and Dad knew about it. You know how families are.'

Joy surged through Jane. So that was the reason Stan had not asked her to go to the dance! She should have known he would have a perfectly good explanation. He wanted to take her, but he had to keep a date he had made before he knew her. It was as simple as that, and she was still Stan's girl. But even so, Jane found she could not forget her unhappiness of the past week.

'I would rather have taken you,' Stan told her. 'Honest. I'm sorry I couldn't. I sure felt awful that day in the hall at school. I felt so awful I couldn't even call you up or anything.'

'It's quite all right,' Jane said stiffly. 'I hope you had a good time,' she repeated.

'Oh, it was all right.' Stan showed no enthusiasm. 'But Bitsy is too short and she got lipstick on my coat and she wore a dumb dress with a narrow skirt and I had to take short steps all evening.'

Well! thought Jane. It just goes to show that boys don't look at things the way girls do. Here I was feeling awkward and unsophisticated beside this Bitsy, the smooth girl from the city.

'She's not like you,' said Stan. 'She laughed at my job. She kept laughing and saying, "Imagine delivering horse meat to *dogs*!" all evening. Maybe it does seem funny to some people, but I like dogs and I like my job.'

Poor Stan, thought Jane tenderly; he sounds so hurt. How thoughtless of Bitsy to make fun of his job.

A car drove past the spot where Jane and Stan were sitting. Jane began to feel uneasy. She did not want it to get around town, and back to her mother and father, that she and Stan had been seen parked in a car. Not even in broad daylight. Her mother would have enough to say about Stan's having a car of his own, even though it could not possibly be called a hot rod, without bringing up the question of parking.

Jane turned to Stan and smiled. 'I know what,' she said. 'Let's go show Julie your car.'

'You're not mad?' he asked, looking down at her.

Jane knew that her answer was important to Stan. 'No, Stan,' she said honestly. 'I'm not mad at you.' But she could not tell him that even though she was not angry, the hurt of the last week was still with her. She was ashamed to admit it.

'Sure?' Stan asked.

'Sure.'

'O.K.,' said Stan, eager to show off his car to someone else. 'Let's go!'

They drove out of the park and down the hill toward Julie's house. The car made loud, popping noises as it went downhill. 'It's just the carburettor,' explained Stan. 'Most cars make that noise going down a steep hill.'

Jane brushed her hair out of her eyes with her new Marcy gesture. 'Oh,' she said resolving to look up 'carburettor' in the dictionary when she got home. Every car had a carburettor, she knew, and she had a vague idea that a carburettor in a car was something like an appendix in a human being, but this was the first time she had met the word in conversation. If Stan wanted to talk about a carburettor, she wanted to find out exactly what it was.

When Stan stopped his car by the kerb in front of Julie's house, Jane reached over to the centre of the steering-wheel and sounded the horn twice, long and loud. Julie and then Buzz appeared at the window. They smiled and waved and in a moment came running down the front steps.

'Say, that's all right" Buzz stood back to admire the Ford. 'She sure looks a lot better than when you got her. Neat but not gaudy.'

'You mean me or the car?' Jane glanced sidelong at Buzz, the way Marcy so often looked at boys.

'The car, of course,' bantered Buzz. 'Anybody can find a girl.'

'Stan, do you mean this car is yours, your very own?' Julie asked.

'That's right,' said Stan proudly. 'I bought it last month, but I had to do a lot of work on it before I could use it.'

Julie stepped up on the running board and leaned over to examine the dashboard. 'And it runs and everything?' she demanded incredulously.

'It sure does,' said Stan. 'A model-A is a little noisier than the cars they make now, but it runs like a top.'

'What's this?' Julie asked, pointing to a cap on the hood in front of the windshield.

'That's the top of the gas tank,' Stan explained.

'In front?' asked Jane.

'On this model,' said Stan.

Buzz opened one side of the hood and bent over to examine the engine. Stan got out of the car and leaned over beside him.

With the two boys half-hidden under the hood, Jane and Julie looked at each other and, without uttering a word, carried on a conversation. Jane's look told Julie that everything was all right. She now understood about Stan and the dance, she was happy to see him again, and she was thrilled about his car. Julie's look told Jane that she was so glad Jane and Stan had things straightened out and that she was both surprised and excited that Buzz had come over to see her so soon after the dance. Both girls silently expressed to each other a feeling of great satisfaction at the way everything had turned out.

'Stan painted his car himself,' said Jane aloud.

'Did he really?' Julie stepped back to admire the paint job.

The two boys came out from under the hood of the car. 'I painted it with a powder puff,' said Stan.

'A powder puff!' laughed Jane. 'Stan, not really!'

'Sure,' said Stan. 'There's a kind of plastic paint for cars, that you put on with a powder puff. You just wipe it on. Of course, I did get a few streaks, and a little dust got in it. And when I tried to paint it in the garage under an electric light, a few moths got into the paint on the hood. See, that's what made these spots.'

'It looks marvellous,' said Julie. 'The spots hardly show, and nobody would ever dream you did it with a powder puff.'

'Look, Julie, it has an old-fashioned rumble seat,' Buzz pointed out. 'That's for you and me to ride in.'

'A real rumble seat!' exclaimed Julie. 'I've always wanted to ride in one. Mother used to ride in one when she was a girl and she's often said what fun it was.'

Stan got into the car and put his foot on the starter. 'We'd better be on our way if I'm going to get Jane to her baby-sitting job on time.'

Buzz stepped up on the running board beside Jane to look at the inside of the car, and as he stood there he looked down at Jane. Then he said, 'Jane, for someone who used to be a scrawny kid who was a terrible cook, you've turned out to be a mighty Purdy girl.'

Jane felt pleased and a little embarrassed by this remark. Buzz was teasing, she knew, but at the same time she was sure he really thought she was pretty. Not knowing how to answer him, she flashed him her new Marcy look.

'A pun is the lowest form of humour,' observed Julie.

Buzz continued to look down at Jane. Then he reached into his pocket and pulled out a fifty-cent piece, which he tossed into the air and deftly caught. 'Stan, I'll give you fifty cents to let me kiss your girl,' he said.

Jane looked at Buzz in astonishment and afterwards she was shocked by her own sudden behaviour. Still feeling like Marcy, she met his challenge. She smiled at him, closed her eyes, and lifted her lips. Buzz leaned over and kissed her lightly on the mouth.

Oh, thought Jane, as his lips touched hers, what have I done? She felt her face flush scarlet as she opened her eyes and saw Buzz, grinning cockily, flip the fifty-cent piece across her lap to Stan, who caught it automatically.

Confused and ashamed, Jane looked down at her hands. She could not think what to do or say. She did not want to look at Buzz and she could not look at Stan. No one spoke.

Unsmiling, Stan kicked the starter button, and the motor roared. As the car began to move, Jane glimpsed Buzz still grinning wickedly at her and, beside him, Julie looking dejectedly after the car, the gaiety she had shown a few minutes before gone out of her. Now I've gone and hurt Julie's feelings, on top of everything else, thought Jane, and I didn't mean to.

'Where to?' asked Stan.

Jane gave him an address in Bayaire Estates. 'I'm sorry, Stan,' she said timidly. 'Really I am.'

'That's O.K.,' said Stan briefly, his eyes on the road.

'I guess I just had a silly impulse. I didn't mean to — to do what I did.'

'Forget it,' said Stan.

He really was angry, Jane realized, and trying to explain wasn't going to help. She could not tell him that she had let Buzz kiss her because she was trying to act like Marcy. It wasn't the sort of thing a boy would understand.

Stan drove on in silence until they came to a bridge that crossed a narrow arm of the bay. In the middle of the bridge Stan stopped his car. Jane put her hand over her eyes to shade them from the brilliant sunlight. 'Why are we stopping?' she asked.

Stan did not answer. With one quick motion he shied Buzz's half dollar across the railing of the bridge and out over the bay. It flashed in the sunlight above the water for an instant before it hit the surface with a plop and sank from sight. 'That takes care of that,' Stan said.

'Why, Stan ...' Jane was startled by his gesture. He's hurt, she thought suddenly. I should have known. Stan was angry, because he was hurt. And with a flash of insight she realized that was the real reason she had let Buzz kiss her. She wanted Stan to feel some of the hurt she had felt. Now she was sorry and ashamed.

When Stan stopped his car in front of the house where Jane was to baby-sit, he glanced at his watch. 'I got you here two minutes late,' he said. 'I'm sorry.'

We seem to be spending the whole morning apologizing to each other, Jane thought, as she got out of the car. He's sorry about the dance. I'm sorry I let Buzz kiss me. He's sorry, because he got me here late. 'That's all right, Stan,' she said, and looked directly at him. 'Are you still mad at me?'

'No,' he said with a weak smile.

'I'm glad, because I really am sorry,' said Jane, and smiled at him. 'Good-bye for now.

'So long, Jane,' he said, without looking at her.

He looks pale under his tan, Jane observed. Actually pale. He must really be upset. She wanted to reassure him, to tell him not to be hurt – that she liked him better than any boy she had ever known – but there was no time to talk. Stan was already driving away.

'Stan!' she called urgently above the noise of the model-A engine. 'Stan, phone me this afternoon!'

She could not hear his answer but it did not matter. A boy who turned pale beneath his tan when another boy kissed her really cared, and a boy who really cared would call. Darling Stan. She was sorry for what she had done, and she could hardly wait for the telephone to ring.

CHAPTER

9

ALTHOUGH baby-sitting with Patsy Scruggs was hard work, Jane was always glad when Mrs Scruggs, the youngest of her customers, called her. Jane felt that the pleasant home the Scruggs had created with ingenuity and not much money was the sort of home she would like to have some day in the shadowy future when she was married. But first she would go to college and have a career. Just what career, she did not know – an airline stewardess, or a writer of advertising copy for a big department store, or perhaps a job at the American embassy in Paris – something like the girls in the pages of *Mademoiselle*, who always managed to be clever about clothes and to be seen in interesting places with men who had crew-cuts.

While little Patsy was engrossed in moving three dolls, a set of blocks, a floppy bear, two old aluminium pans, and a frozen orange-juice can out of her doll buggy and into first one home-upholstered chair and then another, Jane, her thoughts full of Stan, sat smiling dreamily at a framed photograph of Mrs Scruggs, looking young and radiant in her wedding gown. Darling Stan, who was sure to call soon – probably before he started his Doggie Diner route. Stan, who had really wanted to take her to the dance, Stan, who wanted her to be the first girl to ride in his car, Stan, who really cared . . .

Jane let her gaze drift around the room at the odds and

ends of furniture, the unbleached muslin curtains at the windows, the bright unframed prints on the wall, the bookcase made of boards set on stacks of bricks, the worn copy of Dr Benjamin Spock's *Pocket Book of Baby and Child Care*. Mrs Stanley Crandall ... Jane Purdy Crandall ... Stan Crandall, Jr. ...

Patsy, chubby in her corduroy overalls stuffed with nappies and a pair of plastic pants, toddled across the room and plumped her floppy bear and the orange-juice can into Jane's lap.

'Thank you, Patsy,' murmured Jane, and wondered what was showing at the Woodmont Cinema that evening. Or maybe Stan wouldn't ask her to go to the movies this time. Maybe they would just ride around in his car and then go to Nibley's for a milk shake. Patsy, delighted with her game, laughed and made trip after trip to Jane's lap with pans, blocks, and dolls. 'Thank you, Patsy,' said Jane politely each time.

Then the telephone rang. Stan! Jane dumped Patsy's toys to the floor and flew to the kitchen, where she had to throw her shoulder against the door to open it. Doors so often stuck in Bayaire Estates. How thoughtful of Stan to call so soon! He must have remembered he had not mentioned a date for that evening and telephoned the minute he reached home. Jane picked up the receiver. 'Hello,' she said eagerly.

'Hello, Jane.' It was Mrs Scruggs. Jane not only felt let down. She also felt foolish, because of the way she must have sounded when she answered the telephone.

'I'm calling from the dentist's office,' said Mrs Scruggs. 'I forgot to tell you that when you get Patsy's lunch she likes her milk heated.'

'Yes, Mrs Scruggs,' answered Jane. Oh, why couldn't it have been Stan who had called?

'She doesn't like it cold,' continued Mrs Scruggs, 'and she doesn't like it hot, either.'

Hurry, Mrs Scruggs, thought Jane. Stan may be trying to get the line.

'Just heat it enough to take the chill off,' said Patsy's mother. 'I don't like to chill her little stomach with milk right out of the refrigerator.'

'Of course not, Mrs Scruggs.' Hurry and hang up, please!

'But be careful not to get it too hot,' said Mrs Scruggs. 'I wouldn't want her to burn her tongue. And when you heat it, be sure you turn the handle of the pan so she can't pull it off the stove.'

'I'll be careful,' promised Jane.

'And she likes her apple sauce in the dish with the bunnies on the bottom,' Mrs Scruggs went on.

'I'll find it,' said Jane.

'I guess that's all,' said Mrs Scruggs, and finally left the line free for Stan.

Because it was time to fix Patsy's lunch, Jane decided to move the little girl into the kitchen with her. She did not like to leave Patsy in the living-room alone, because she was never sure what mischief her small mind might devise. 'Come on, Patsy,' she coaxed. 'Let's go into the kitchen and fix some nice lunch.'

Agreeably Patsy pushed her doll buggy into the kitchen and removed from it a box, which she dumped on to the floor. Spools of all sizes rolled across the linoleum.

'Patsy, you're not much help,' remarked Jane as she looked around the kitchen. Mrs Scruggs had done everything possible to make the room childproof. The handles of the gas stove had been removed and set out of reach of little hands. Yardsticks had been run through the rows of drawer pulls so that no drawer could be opened without first pulling out a yardstick. The lower cupboards and the refrigerator door were tied shut with lengths of clothesline rope.

Patsy threw a spool across the kitchen, and Jane sighed. It was here that she had to prepare lunch. 'Patsy, how would you like to sit in your high chair while I fix you some nice lunch?' At least she would be near the telephone while she worked.

'No!' said Patsy stubbornly, and hurled another spool across the kitchen.

Jane realized she had made a mistake. She should have told Patsy, not asked her. Oh, well, what difference did it make whether Patsy was underfoot or in her high chair? She could watch the little girl while she waited for Stan's call. Jane untied the refrigerator door and removed, according to Mrs Scrugg's instructions, the milk, some cooked green beans, a bowl containing chopped liver and bacon, some apple sauce, and some cheese for her own sandwich. Then she tied the door shut again.

Next Jane untied a cupboard to look for pans, but the cupboard was full of platters and casseroles. She tied it shut again and untied another cupboard, from which she removed two small pans for heating the meat and the vegetable. She tied it shut, remembered she must heat the milk, untied it, removed another pan, and tied it shut again.

Patsy rolled some spools across the floor. Stepping carefully, Jane carried the pans to the stove. Then she examined the knobs that had been removed and fitted them into place on the front of the stove. She stepped back across the kitchen and pulled a yardstick out of a row of deep drawers. The first metal-lined drawer was filled with flour, the second contained sugar, and in the third she found a loaf of bread, which she took out and placed on the draining-board. Then she remembered that the butter was still in the refrigerator, so she untied the door, took out the butter, and tied the door again.

The telephone rang. Stan! cried Jane's heart, as she stepped on a spool, caught herself on the edge of the draining-board, and picked up the receiver. 'Hello?' she said, cautiously this time.

'Oh, hello, Marilyn,' said a woman's voice. 'I just wanted to tell you I went downtown this morning, and Penney's is having the most wonderful sale of children's corduroy overalls. You know – the kind with snaps. These were so cute, because the knees were padded and quilted in designs like ducks and kittens, and when I saw them I thought, I must call Marilyn, because I'm sure she'll want to buy some for Patsy.'

'Excuse me,' said Jane, her voice heavy with disappointment. 'This is not Mrs Scruggs. This is her sitter.'

'Oh. Excuse *me*,' apologized the woman. 'Isn't that funny? I could have sworn it was Marilyn Scruggs who answered.'

'Could I take a message?' asked Jane, wilted because the call was not from Stan. By now he had started the Doggie Diner route, but he could easily telephone from a drugstore between stops.

'No, thanks,' said the woman. 'I'll call back.'

Once more the line was free for Stan. Jane heard the sound of a drawer opening behind her and turned just in time to see Patsy fill both hands with sugar and fling it on to the kitchen floor. She bubbled forth a laugh of sheer delight as she slid her little feet across the floor through the gritty sugar.

'Patsy!' cried Jane, and then told herself she might as well save her breath. It was her own fault. She should have remembered to replace the yardstick and she should not have turned her back for one instant. She would not think about the telephone any more. Then it would be sure to ring.

Somehow, Jane managed to pick up the spools, sweep up the sugar, prepare Patsy's lunch, install her in her high chair, and get her started eating, partly with a spoon and partly with her fingers. With one hand Jane ate a cheese sandwich and drank a glass of milk and with the other she assisted Patsy in finding her mouth, and all the time she wondered where Stan was on his route. The Doberman's house? The boxer's house? Or had he reached the grey poodle's house yet?

'Blah, blah, black sheep,' said Patsy, dribbling apple sauce down her chin.

'Have you any wool?' prompted Jane.

Patsy squished apple sauce around in her mouth and studied Jane. 'No,' she answered, and Jane laughed.

When Jane finished her own lunch she used both hands to help Patsy get the apple sauce into her mouth and find the bunnies in the bottom of her dish. She was about to wipe the little girl's face with a damp washcloth and find a rag for mopping up the food spilled on the floor when the telephone rang again. This time it *had* to be Stan. The third time was the charm. Jane snatched up the telephone and said breathlessly, 'Hello?'

'Hello, Jane,' said Mrs Scruggs. 'I'm just leaving the dentist's office and I'll be home in about fifteen minutes. Is everything all right?'

'Everything's fine, Mrs Scruggs,' answered Jane, disappointed a third time. 'Patsy has just finished her lunch.'

'I want to talk,' cried Patsy from her high chair.

'Let her say hello,' said Mrs Scruggs. 'She loves to talk on the telephone.'

With a sigh, Jane plucked the chubby little girl from her high chair and carried her to the telephone. 'Say hello to Mommy,' she directed.

Patsy grasped the telephone with both hands. 'I'm fine,' she shouted into the mouthpiece, before her mother had time to speak to her. 'I'm fine.'

It took Jane several minutes to separate Patsy from the telephone – the minutes, she was sure, in which Stan was trying to reach her. She dampened the washcloth again under the faucet, and while she wiped apple sauce from Patsy's face and from the telephone she decided Stan might not want to call her at a stranger's house. Perhaps he was waiting until later in the afternoon, when he was sure she would be at home.

It was not long before the front door opened and Mrs Scruggs came in. 'Hello, Jane,' she said, snatching Patsy into her arms. 'How's Mommy's 'ittle s'eetheart?' she cried. 'How's Mommy's 'ittle s'eetheart? Have you been a good girl while Mommy was away?'

Patsy laughed and buried her face in her mother's neck. Mrs Scruggs set the little girl down and reached for her purse. Jane glanced at her watch and saw that she had been sitting only an hour and a half. It had seemed longer. Mrs Scruggs handed Jane seventy-five cents and Jane thanked her. The Scruggs, Jane knew, did not have much money for baby-sitters.

'Mrs Scruggs, if anyone telephones for me, would you say I'll be home in about five minutes?' Jane asked.

'Of course, Jane.' Mrs Scruggs smiled understandingly. 'Especially if someone is a boy.'

Jane left as quickly as she could and all but ran home, because she did not want to be away from a telephone an instant longer than necessary. When she entered her own house she found her mother telephoning her grocery list. 'A quart of mayonnaise . . . a large bottle of vanilla . . . a box of Kleenex . . . oh, all right, send me two . . . a large box of oatmeal . . . yes, the quick-cooking kind . . .'

Hurry, Mom, thought Jane. Stan may be trying to call me between deliveries this very instant. He won't have much time.

'Do you have any nice cross-rib roasts?' Mrs Purdy went on. 'Good. Send me one about four, no, about five pounds . . . and a pound of lean bacon. . . . Let me see. Yes, I think that's all for today.'

Thank goodness, thought Jane, as her mother hung up. Now Stan could reach her.

'Hello, Jane,' said Mrs Purdy, her hand still on the telephone. 'I know I forgot something. What could it be?'

'I don't know, Mom. It sounded as if you ordered everything,' answered Jane, wishing her mother would get away from the telephone.

'Oh, I know.' Jane's mother dialled a number, as if she had nothing to do the rest of the day. 'Hello, this is Mrs

Purdy again. I'm sorry, but I forgot the most important item on my list. A pound of lamb's liver for the cat ... yes, that's right, we can't forget him. He's the most important member of the family. At least that's what he thinks.' She laughed comfortably before she hung up.

It's about time, thought Jane. Now maybe Stan can reach me. She went into her room and pulled her back-scratcher out from under the pile of sweaters in the drawer and tied it to the edge of her mirror once more. She changed into her yellow cotton dress, in case Stan dropped by instead of telephoning, and tried brushing her hair down close to her head to see how she would look with a sleek new haircut. Awful, she decided. Sort of forlorn and underfed. She fluffed up her hair again and renewed her lipstick, carefully outlining her mouth with the lipstick brush. Then she got out her paper sack of yarn and cast on seventy-six stitches to start an Argyle sock.

'Jane, would you go out and move the hose?' Mrs Purdy asked. 'It's been running on the fuchsias long enough.'

'O.K.,' said Jane. She left the front door open, in case the telephone should ring, and ran down the front steps. She turned off the water, moved the sprinkler to another corner of the lawn, turned on the water, and ran back into the house. The telephone had not rung.

As the afternoon wore on, Jane began to feel that something must be wrong. Stan had been delayed on his route. He had had a flat tyre. Or, as sometimes happened, the boxer had followed the truck so far he had been obliged to return the dog to its home and tie it up. Or maybe the telephone was out of order. Or the other party on their line was talking. Quietly Jane slipped to the telephone and slid the receiver off the hook. The dial tone buzzed busily in her ear. With a sigh, she replaced the receiver. She wished the line had been out of order. Then she would know why Stan had not called. I guess a watched telephone never rings, she thought gloomily, as she went back to her knitting. Doubt began to creep into her mind. Maybe she had misunderstood. She had not actually heard Stan say he would telephone. Perhaps she had made him so angry he would never call her again. Perhaps – but she could not bring herself to believe it.

At a quarter to five the telephone rang, startling Jane so that she dropped six stitches and tripped on the edge of the rug before she could answer it. 'Hello?' She tried to keep eagerness out of her voice.

'I have good news for you!' exclaimed a man's voice enthusiastically.

Jane was surprised. Good news for her? Who could be calling with good news for her?

'You have been chosen to receive one of our special gift offers of one nine-by-twelve tinted photograph with any order of ten dollars or more at Sherwood's Photography Studio!' The voice bubbled with enthusiasm.

'No, thank you. I'm not interested,' said Jane dully, and hung up. He has good news for me, she thought ironically. That's what *he* thinks. The only good news she wanted was Stan's call. The minutes began to drag.

By five-thirty Jane knew that Stan had finished his route long ago and was home by now. She had to face the unpleasant truth. Stan was not going to telephone. She could make excuses no longer. She felt tired, let down, worn out by anticipation. Wearily she set the table for her mother, her thoughts still filled with Stan. The happiness she had felt earlier in the day was gone, replaced by doubt and confusion. She laid a fresh napkin at each place. She must have been mistaken about Stan's set look, the pallor beneath his tan. He had not been hurt at all. He was angry and disgusted with her for having acted like a silly, impetuous fifteen-year-old. And she did not blame him one bit. He had been so sorry about the dance and had wanted her to be the first girl to ride in his car, and then she had acted that way. How dumb can I get, she asked herself bitterly, just exactly how dumb?

Jane ate her dinner in silence. Sir Puss, who had dry adobe mud clinging to his paws, walked with a clicking sound across the bare floor between the living-room and dining-room rugs.

'That cat makes entirely too much noise pussy-footing around this house,' said Mr Purdy.

Jane responded to her father's joke with a wan smile.

Mr Purdy tried again. 'Well, I hear the horse-meat king came to call this morning,' he said jovially.

'Pop, please !' implored Jane. 'Mom, would you excuse me? I really don't care for any dessert.'

'Yes, of course, Jane,' said Mrs Purdy.

'*Now* what's wrong with her?' Jane heard her father ask as she fled the room.

'The same old thing,' answered Mrs Purdy. 'Love.'

You'd think people who had been young once would be more understanding, Jane thought, as she sat down on her bed and picked up her knitting. Slowly she pulled out the needles and one by one began to undo the stitches she had knit that afternoon. Apathetically she wound the frayed yarn into a ball. She did not know what to do now.

Jane wondered what she would do about Stan if she

were some other girl. If she were the kind of girl who went to school with her hair in pin curls, she would probably telephone the disc jockey at Station KWOO and ask him to play *Love Me on Monday* to Stan from Jane. If she were intellectual like Liz, she would probably say that dancing and riding around in a model-A Ford were boring or middlebrow or something, and spend the evening writing hokkus for Manuscript. Or if she were the earnest type she could write a letter to Teen Corner in the newspaper. The letter would begin, 'Dear Ann Benedict, I wonder if you could help me solve a problem. Recently I met a boy . . .' If she were the cashmere-sweater type, like Marcy, she would date several other boys and forget Stan.

But Jane was not any of these girls. She was Jane Purdy, an ordinary girl who was no type at all. She was neither earnest nor intellectual, and she certainly wasn't the kind of girl the boys flocked around. She was just a girl who liked to have a good time, who made reasonably good grades at school, and who still liked a boy who had once liked her. There was nothing wrong with that.

All right, then why didn't she act that way, Jane asked herself, instead of trying to toss her hair around like Marcy the minute she got to ride in a boy's car with the top down. If she had not been trying to act like Marcy, she would never have closed her eyes and lifted her lips for Buzz to kiss.

Jane sat toying with the ball of yarn and thinking about Marcy. Why, she did not even like the girl. Not really. She did not like girls who acted bored and who made other girls feel uncomfortable. She liked girls who were friendly and interested in others. Then why, Jane asked herself, did she try to act like someone she did not like? Maybe she didn't have a lot of sun streaks in her hair or a drawer full of cashmere sweaters, but a nice boy like Stan had liked her once and Buzz had wanted to kiss her, so she was certainly as attractive as most girls at school. All she lacked was confidence. She didn't know why she hadn't thought of it before.

From now on, Jane resolved, she would be Jane Purdy and nobody else. She would stop feeling like Miss Muffet around Marcy and she would no longer feel fluffy and not very bright when she talked to Liz. From now on she would be confident. When she saw Stan she would act glad to see him, because no matter what had happened that was the way Jane Purdy felt. After all, Stan had liked her when she was baby-sitting with Sandra and when she walked through Chinatown with him, and she had been herself both those times. Maybe if she continued to be herself, Stan would like her again. And if he didn't, there was nothing she could do about it. Jane was filled with a wonderful feeling of relief at having made this decision. That was that. Period.

Jane tossed the ball of yarn on to her bed and, humming the Woodmont High victory song, went into the living-room, where she dropped into the nearest chair. 'Hi,' she said amiably to her father and mother.

'Welcome,' said Mr Purdy over his evening paper. 'Have you decided to join the family once more?'

'Oh, Pop, don't be silly,' said Jane.

'I thought you were going out with the horse-meat king.'

'Not tonight,' said Jane casually, and picked up a magazine. 'I guess the horse-meat king is doing something else.' The telephone rang, but she made no move to answer it.

She was not expecting any calls, and she found it restful after the day she had spent.

'You get it, Jane,' said Mrs Purdy.

'O.K.,' answered Jane, and walked leisurely into the hall to pick up the receiver.

'Hello. Jane?' Julie's excited voice sounded muffled and far away.

'Julie, where are you?' Jane asked. 'You sound as if you were at the bottom of a well, or something.'

'In the hall closet at Greg's.'

'In the hall closet? What on earth for?' Jane demanded. 'And what are you doing at Greg's in the first place?'

'Buzz brought me over, and we're listening to records with a bunch of kids. Their telephone has a long cord, and I just had to talk to you where nobody could hear me, so I took it into the hall closet,' Julie explained. Then she said something Jane could not understand.

'Julie, I can't hear you,' complained Jane.

'It's dark in here and a coat or something fell down on me,' Julie told her.

Jane had something she was anxious to get off her mind. 'Julie, I am terribly sorry about – what I did this morning. You what what. I can't talk much now,' she said, aware of her parents in the next room.

'That's strange,' Jane heard her father say. 'Usually she is good for a couple of hours.'

'It's all right, Jane,' said Julie. 'I mean, after all, Buzz asked me for a date tonight, and that's what counts. But that isn't what I called about. Jane, did anybody tell you about Stan?' Julie sounded eager and excited, as if she had important news.

Stan! What could have happened to Stan? 'No. Nobody called. Is something wrong?' Jane asked anxiously.

'Late this afternoon he was rushed to the hospital and had his appendix out!' Obviously Julie relished breaking this news.

'In the hospital?' Jane was stunned. Stan in the hospital? He couldn't be. Not Stan. But he must be, if Julie said so. 'Is he all right?' she asked at last.

'Yes. Buzz talked to his mother a little while ago, and she said everything was fine,' answered Julie.

'Oh. That's good!' Jane's mind was not really on what she was saying. She was seeing everything in a new light. This was the reason Stan had not called! An appendix, of all things! He must have been pale under his tan that morning, not because he was angry, not because he was hurt, but because he had a pain in his appendix!

'Look, I've got to go now,' said Julie. 'It's hot in here and the others might miss me.'

'Thanks for calling,' said Jane absently. 'Have fun.' She sat staring at the cover of the telephone book. Stan in the hospital. Stan, pale and still in a narrow white bed, stuff dripping out of a bottle into a vein in his arm, nurses hovering over him, taking his temperature, feeling his pulse . . .

And how, Jane asked herself, does Jane Purdy, the confident Jane Purdy, behave when the boy she likes, who is angry with her (she *thought* – now she wasn't sure), is in the hospital with his appendix out?

CHAPTER

10

FOR the next three days Jane wondered what she should do about Stan. She looked over the get-well cards in Woodmont's stationery store, but neither the sentimental cards adorned with roses and violets nor the cards printed with elephants or kittens and silly verses seemed exactly right for a special boy. She considered sending Stan a note and even wrote on her best letter paper, 'Dear Stan, I am sorry to hear about your operation. I hope you get well soon.' Then she sat nibbling the end of her fountain pen. She could not think of another thing to say.

Jane reread what she had written. It would be the right message, she decided, to put on a card enclosed with a gift. But what gift could a girl send to a boy who had his appendix out? A book, perhaps, but she did not know what Stan liked to read. She did not want to send something he would not enjoy and then have him feel he had to read it just to be polite. Besides, she did not know how to get a book to a boy in a hospital. She did not want to visit him, because he would probably be surrounded by his mother and father and sisters and a few aunts and uncles and cousins, and he would have to introduce her to everyone and that would be embarrassing, especially if he was angry with her.

Flowers? Jane chewed the end of her pen and considered this idea. She could go to the flower shop, select some flowers, write a few words on a card, and ask the florist to deliver her gift for her. Stan would know she was sorry about his bad luck and they would not have to meet in case he didn't want to see her. But flowers to a boy? Well, why not? Anyone in a hospital ought to enjoy receiving flowers. The more Jane considered sending flowers – masculine flowers, of course – to Stan, the better she liked the idea. It would be a friendly but not over-eager thing to do. And she had resolved to act like Jane Purdy and nobody else, hadn't she? No matter how Stan felt towards her, she was truly sorry to hear that he was in the hospital and she really did hope he would get well soon. Well, all right then. She would send Stan some flowers.

But a hint of doubt still lingered in Jane's mind, because she had never known a girl who liked a boy who had his appendix out, and so she had no precedent to follow. Jane did not like to ask her mother's advice about anything, because she almost never liked the advice her mother gave, but this time she felt she had to consult someone.

Jane found her mother reading a magazine in a deck chair in the back yard. Sir Puss, who always sought the most fragrant spot, was sunning himself in the middle of the herb garden. 'Mom,' she said, eyeing with disapproval her mother's bare legs, 'do you think it would be all right if I sent Stan some flowers at the hospital?'

Mrs Purdy looked up from her magazine. 'Why, I think it would be a very nice thing to do. The begonias are about gone, but there are some pretty chrysanthemums on the other side of the garage.'

'I'll go look at them,' said Jane noncommittally.

'If you want to pick some I could drive you over to the hospital,' suggested Mrs Purdy. 'It's too late for visiting hours, but you could leave them at the desk and a nurse would take them to Stan.'

'Not right now,' murmured Jane vaguely, as she walked around the garage on the pretence of examining her father's chrysanthemums. Imagine her mother thinking she could just go out in the yard and pick a bunch of flowers and take them to Stan at the hospital! If that wasn't just like Mom. She probably expected her to wrap the home-grown flowers in a newspaper or in a piece of waxed paper from the roll in the kitchen and then walk into the lobby of the Cronk Memorial Hospital with a bouquet that looked too loving-hands-at-home for words. The nurses would probably laugh at her. And what did Mom expect her to use for a card? A piece of notepaper? That was the trouble with Mom. She meant well, but she just didn't understand.

Jane lifted the head of one of her father's chrysanthemums, a great spidery blossom in a delicate shade of pink. It was fragile and lovely, but honestly, what was Mom thinking of? Pink flowers for Stan! A boy should have masculine flowers, like geraniums or something. No, not geraniums. They were too common. But some kind of masculine flower.

The conversation with her mother had cleared up one point for Jane, however. It was perfectly proper for a girl to send flowers to a boy who was in the hospital. Tomorrow, after school, she would walk confidently into De Luca's Flower Shop next door to Nibley's, select some masculine flowers, write her message on a proper florist's card, and get Mr De Luca to deliver the bouquet to the Cronk Memorial Hospital. What could be simpler?

Twenty-four hours later Jane, who had never before

sent flowers to anyone, paused in front of De Luca's Flower Shop. One window displayed a bouquet of white stock and chrysanthemums suitable for a wedding. The other was filled with philodendron, its split leaves the size of dinner plates, climbing a moss-covered stick. Confidently Jane opened the door and stepped into the cool shop.

'May I help you?' asked Mr De Luca, who was wearing a green smock.

'Yes, please.' Jane glanced around at the displays of vases, figurines, and potted plants. 'I want to send some flowers to someone in the hospital.'

'We have some nice yellow roses,' said the florist, reaching into the refrigerator at the back of the shop and producing a container of roses. 'We can give you a nice arrangement of a dozen and a half roses tied with yellow satin ribbon and set in a round glass bowl for five dollars.'

Dubiously Jane looked at the roses. They were too pretty. It was difficult to believe that such perfect blooms had once been attached to bushes with roots growing in soil and manure. No, hothouse roses with a satin ribbon were not right for Stan, Jane decided. 'I don't think that is exactly what I had in mind,' she told the florist.

'We have some nice chrysanthemums today,' suggested Mr De Luca, pointing to a container of tousle-headed blooms, the kind Jane hoped to wear to a football game some day when she was in college.

'No, I don't think so,' said Jane.

'Or how about these?' asked the florist, pointing to some spidery pink chrysanthemums.

Jane felt that these blooms were not nearly so pretty as those in her own back yard. 'Well . . . no, I guess not.' She was beginning to be embarrassed. By now Mr De Luca must be impatient with her.

'Are the flowers for a new mother?' asked the florist. 'Perhaps if I had some idea ...'

'Oh, no,' said Jane hastily. 'They are for a – a man.'

'I see.' Mr De Luca's voice was grave, as if he realized the importance of the occasion. 'A young man?'

'Sort of. I wanted something more ... well, something more masculine.'

'Yes, of course,' agreed Mr De Luca. 'Let me see,' he muttered to himself, 'masculine flowers.'

Jane began to feel uncomfortable. She had not realized it would be so difficult to select flowers.

'Would a nice dish garden do?' the florist asked helpfully. 'We have some made up with ivy, variegated peperomia, and white-veined fittonia.'

Jane, used to the lovely flowers her father grew in their yard, decided that plants without blossoms did not appeal to her. 'No, I want to send flowers,' she insisted, wishing she was not so much trouble to wait on.

'I have it!' exclaimed the florist. 'How about glads?' He reached into the refrigerator and brought out a couple of stalks of pink gladiolas and held them up for Jane's inspection. 'Nothing sissy about glads, is there?'

Jane scrutinized the blossoms on the long straight stems. They were pink, but not a delicate, feminine pink. They were more of a flaming sunset pink. Yes, Jane decided, gladiolas could probably be called masculine flowers.

'With a few delphiniums and some ferns they make a nice arrangement,' said Mr De Luca hopefully. 'I can give you a dozen glads, half a dozen delphiniums, and throw in some ferns for three dollars and a half.'

'All right. I'll take them,' agreed Jane, glad to have made a decision at last. She dug into her coin purse for some of her baby-sitting money, which she handed across the counter. 'And would you please send them to the Cronk Memorial Hospital?'

'I'm sorry, miss,' said the florist. 'We don't deliver under five dollars.'

'Oh.' Jane was taken aback by this news. Still, it was only about four blocks to the hospital, and she could easily walk over with the flowers and leave them at the information desk to be sent up to Stan's room, the way her mother had suggested. The flowers would be wrapped in proper green florist's paper and would not have the loving-hands-at-home look of flowers picked in the garden and wrapped in waxed paper, so she would have no reason to feel ashamed of them. 'I'll take them anyway,' said Jane. 'I can carry them over to the hospital.'

'You can be writing a card if you like,' suggested Mr De Luca. 'I'll have the flowers ready for you in a few minutes.'

Jane sat down at the desk in the corner of the shop and chose a plain white card. She wrote, 'Dear Stan, I am sorry to hear about your operation. I hope you get well soon. Jane.' Then she carefully wrote *Stanley Crandall* on the envelope and was about to put the card inside when she realized her message was all wrong. It was too stiff and prim, too Miss Muffetish. She tore the card into bits and dropped them into the wastebasket. On a second card she wrote, 'Sorry to hear about your bad luck. Hope you get well soon. Jane.' That was better. It was friendly and casual and not so prim.

'Here we are,' announced Mr De Luca.

Jane turned from the desk to look and it occurred to her that it was a good thing she was sitting down. Otherwise, the shock of seeing her flowers might have been too much for her. They were not discreetly wrapped in green paper, as she had anticipated. The flaming sunset gladiolas, the intense blue delphiniums, and the ferns were arranged in a foil-covered container ornamented with a blue ribbon. The stalks of flowers stuck out like the spikes on the crown of the Statue of Liberty, and the spaces between were filled with asparagus fern. The whole lurid thing was at least three feet across.

'Made up real nice, didn't it?' Mr De Luca adjusted a fern and stood back to admire his work.

'Uh . . . yes,' answered Jane. Now what was she going to do? She couldn't tell the florist she had changed her mind after she had paid him and he had gone to all that work and looked so pleased with what he had done. For a frantic moment Jane considered rushing out of the shop, never to return. She couldn't do that either, and she did not know what she could do except deliver the monstrous bouquet. Good old Jane Purdy, she thought grimly. She means well, but she always manages to do the wrong thing. She has a real talent for it.

Since she had made up her mind to be herself and since she was the kind of person who always did the wrong thing, Jane decided she might as well make the best of it and start out by delivering the flowers to Stan. That was exactly what she would do. She would see this thing through if it was the last thing she did. Jane felt a kind of triumph at this decision. What if she did run into someone who knew her? What if the kids from school did tease her?

She would find an answer for them. A little confidence was all she needed.

'Is something wrong?' asked Mr De Luca. 'You don't like it?'

'It's very pretty,' answered Jane faintly. And it *was* pretty in a gaudy way. The blossoms were fresh, the blue bow was jaunty, the colours harmonized. It was just that it was so big. Jane told herself she might as well get started. She couldn't just sit there all day. In spite of her decision she rose reluctantly and lifted her flowers from the counter. 'Thank you for – for arranging the flowers,' she said as she peered through the foliage at Mr De Luca.

'Here, let me open the door for you,' said the florist. The bouquet was too wide for the door, so Jane walked sideways out of the shop.

Jane had to pass Nibley's on her way to Cronk Memorial Hospital and, as she had expected, a gang from Woodmont High was congregated in front of the entrance. A gang of boys, she gathered from their voices. And this time she was not going to let anybody tease her, she told herself severely. She would show them. She would remember she was Jane Purdy and no one else. Maybe she was doing the wrong thing, but that was the way she was.

'Hey, look what's coming!' she heard a boy's voice exclaim, and there was a hoot of laughter from the crowd.

'What is it?' asked another boy.

'It has a skirt and legs and feet. It must be half human,' said another boy.

'Yes, and the legs aren't bad.' Jane recognized Buzz's voice. She had tried to avoid Buzz since he had kissed her, but this time she didn't care if he did see her. Ha, she'd show him. That wolf, junior grade.

Jane lowered her bouquet and peered over the blossoms. 'Hi,' she said.

Buzz grinned at her, that annoying grin he had flashed at her since the morning he had kissed her. Jane felt her face flush in spite of herself. 'What do you think you're doing, hiding behind that?' Buzz asked.

'I'm taking this to Stan, at the hospital,' Jane said coolly. 'Is that all right with you?'

'You call that thing a bouquet?' asked Buzz.

'No, I don't call it a bouquet,' Jane answered pertly. 'I call it camouflage.'

This time everyone laughed at Buzz. Score one for me, thought Jane. The door of Nibley's opened and Marcy, followed by Greg, walked out.

Jane did not wait for Marcy to make her feel like Miss Muffet. 'Hi, Marcy,' she said. 'Look at the flowers I'm taking to Stan. Did you ever see anything so enormous in all your life?'

'Wow!' exclaimed Greg with a friendly laugh. 'I'll bet he'll be surprised.'

Jane giggled. 'Not half as much as I was when I saw it.'

'You mean you're taking Stan flowers after he took someone else to the dance?' asked Marcy.

Meow to you, too, Marcy, thought Jane, but she said, 'Why not? He could hardly break a date he had made before he met me, could he?'

Marcy looked surprised. 'No, I suppose not,' she had to admit.

Score two for me, thought Jane, and said sweetly, 'Stan told me all about it.'

'Oh,' said Marcy.

That takes care of that, thought Jane. Good-bye, Miss

Muffet. Good-bye forever. 'And now if you gentlemen will step aside, I'll be on my way,' she said to the crowd of boys.

The boys parted, and Jane saw Julie and Liz approaching Nibley's. 'Jane!' cried Julie in horror. 'Are you ... you're not —'

'Yes,' answered Jane calmly. 'I am.'

'Why didn't you have them delivered?' whispered Julie, when she had reached Jane's side.

'Because they won't deliver anything under five dollars,' said Jane, 'and being me, I didn't find it out until it was too late.'

'Don't you want me to go with you?' asked Julie.

'No, thank you, Julie,' answered Jane. Actually, Jane would have been grateful for her friend's company, but she had made up her mind to see this thing through and she was going to see it through without any help from anyone. 'I can peek through this, you know. I don't need someone to guide me. But thanks anyway for the moral support.'

'It's a pretty bouquet,' said Julie, 'even if it is sort of big.'

'You know, you remind me of Birnam wood,' remarked Liz.

'What's Birnam wood?' Jane wanted to know.

'Haven't you read *Macbeth*?' Liz sounded superior.

Jane stood her ground and refused to let Liz make her feel fluffy and not very bright. 'No, I've only had *As You Like It* and *Julius Caesar*,' she answered, and it occurred to her that high-school students, except intellectuals like Liz, always said they had had Shakespeare's plays instead of saying they had studied them.

'You'll get *Macbeth* next year,' explained Greg, making Shakespeare sound like the measles. 'This bunch of soldiers broke off a lot of boughs and branches and stuff in a place called Birnam wood and held them up in front of them for camouflage and crept up on Macbeth's castle. It looked like the wood was advancing.'

Jane laughed. 'That's me. I'm creeping up on Cronk Memorial Hospital.'

'Say, I'll walk over with you,' offered a boy in a second-year letter man's sweater.

'No, thank you,' said Jane, and smiled at the crowd. ''Bye now.'

'Funny I've never noticed her before,' she heard the letter man remark as she left.

A delicious feeling of satisfaction flowed through Jane as she proceeded behind her flowers toward the hospital. She had been herself, Jane Purdy, and no one else. It hadn't been easy, but it had worked! People turned to stare at her, cars tooted at her, but Jane did not care. She only smiled and went on her way, past the shops, down a shaded street, and up the steps of the Cronk Memorial Hospital.

Inside, everyone – doctors, nurses, visitors – stopped to stare at Jane and to smile as if highly amused. Her ordeal was nearly ended. Jane propelled her bouquet across the lobby to the information desk where, free of it at last, she set the bouquet on the counter. 'I would like to leave this for Stanley Crandall,' she said.

The attendant, obviously trying to suppress a smile, flipped through a file of cards. 'I'm sorry, but Mr Crandall was discharged this morning,' she informed Jane.

'So soon?' asked Jane in dismay.

'Yes, we don't keep them long nowadays,' explained the attendant, glancing at the card again. 'You can reach him at 17 Poppy Lane.'

Jane's confidence wavered. '17 Poppy Lane,' she repeatedly blankly. That was only three blocks away. There was nothing to do now but go ahead and deliver the flowers to his house. If she didn't, Stan was sure to hear about them from the crowd at school and wonder why he had never received them. Stifling a sudden desire to giggle, she picked up her flowers once more. Here goes Birnam wood again, she thought, and advanced behind her bouquet across the lobby, out of the hospital, and down the street toward Poppy Lane.

When Jane reached Stan's block, a stocky little girl about eight years old, who had been roller-skating aimlessly up and down the sidewalk, darted up to Jane. 'What are you carrying that for?' she demanded.

'Because,' answered Jane.

'Because why?' persisted the girl.

'I'm taking them to a sick friend,' Jane told the child.

'My brother had his appendix out. He just came home from the hospital today,' the girl informed Jane.

Jane lowered her bouquet for a better look at this child, who had brown pigtails, a dirty face, and Stan's grey-green eyes.

'Say!' exclaimed Stan's little sister. 'I'll bet you're taking all those flowers to my brother!'

Jane felt she might as well admit it. 'Yes,' she said. 'I am.'

The child's face lit up with excitement. 'Gee!' she exclaimed, and darted off, her skates going *ching-chung* against the cement. At number seventeen, she turned and clomped up the steps. 'Hey, Mom,' she yelled, as she threw open the front door. 'Come quick! Somebody's bringing flowers to Stan, and it's a girl!'

Jane squelched an urge to fling her flowers into the gutter and run. It was too late for that. With her cheeks flaming, she marched bravely up the steps of Stan's house and reached the front door just as Mrs Crandall appeared. There she was, face to face with Stan's mother. From behind her floral screen Jane wanted to faint, disappear in a puff of smoke, drop dead, anything to get out of this awful situation. Instead she stared, as if stricken, over the spikes of gladiolas at this unknown person, Stan's mother.

Mrs Crandall, a comfortable-looking woman, smiled reassuringly at Jane. 'What lovely flowers!' she exclaimed. 'And how thoughtful of you to bring them to Stan.'

'I – I meant him to have them at the hospital,' said Jane shyly. 'I didn't know he would leave so soon.'

'They don't keep patients long in hospitals after an operation these days,' explained Mrs Crandall. 'Here, let me take the flowers.'

Gratefully Jane surrendered her burden.

'Stan is taking a nap right now,' Mrs Crandall went on, as if receiving a gaudy floral piece from a strange girl were not at all unusual, 'but won't you come in?'

'Well, no – thank you,' said Jane uncertainly. 'I think I had better be going home. My – my mother is expecting me.'

Mrs Crandall smiled warmly at Jane across the flowers. 'You must be Jane Purdy,' she said.

'Yes, I am,' Jane admitted, and wondered what Stan had said about her to his family.

'Stan has spoken of you so often,' said Mrs Crandall. 'You must come over and have dinner with us sometime.'

'I – I would love to,' stammered Jane, pleased and embarrassed by this unexpected invitation. She only hoped that Stan would be pleased too.

'Boy, does Stan like you!' the little sister informed Jane. 'He always shines his shoes for about an hour before he goes to see you!'

'Mitzi!' exclaimed Mrs Crandall with a laugh.

'Well, he does,' persisted Mitzi. 'He says –'

'Mitzi!' Mrs Crandall's voice held a warning.

Jane felt her face flush even redder. 'Tell Stan everybody misses him at school,' she said, and turned to leave.

'Thank you so much for the flowers, Jane,' said Mrs Crandall. 'It was thoughtful of you to bring them to Stan, and I know he'll be pleased.'

'I hope so,' said Jane, more at ease with this pleasant woman, who looked as if she understood how difficult it was to be fifteen. 'Good-bye, Mrs Crandall.'

'Good-bye, Jane.'

'Good-bye,' called Mitzi, as Jane walked down the steps. 'Golly, Mom, did you ever see such a *big* bunch of flowers.'

Jane walked sedately down the street and around the corner from Poppy Lane, but she did not feel at all sedate. She wanted to run and skip and shout. Her ordeal was over. She had not acted like Miss Muffet when the gang from school had tried to tease her. Mrs Crandall had been friendly and had not laughed at her and, best of all, she had learned that Stan liked her enough to talk about her to his family. Maybe she had, in her usual way, done all the wrong things, but everything had turned out all right.

Maybe that was the way things were when a girl was fifteen. And Stan shined his shoes before he came to see her. His sister said so. Darling Stan in his shiny shoes!

'Hi, Mom,' Jane greeted her mother cheerfully, as she walked into the house.

Mrs Purdy looked up from sewing and smiled. 'Did you have a good day?'

'M-m-m. Good and bad. Mostly good, though.' Jane lifted Sir Puss from the chair in which he was napping and buried her face in his tabby fur. 'How's the old pussy cat?' she asked him. 'Hm-m? How's the old pussy cat today?'

Sir Puss struggled free and leaped to the floor, where he glared at Jane and then began meticulously to wash himself, as if the touch of her hands had soiled him. 'You're a spoiled old thing,' Jane told him, as the telephone rang. 'I'll get it, Mom,' she said, and went into the hall. 'Hello?' She spoke blithely, for once not caring who was on the line.

'Hi, there.' It was Stan.

'Oh – hello,' answered Jane eagerly. It was so good to hear his voice once more.

'I want to thank you for the flowers,' said Stan. 'They're sure pretty.'

'I'm glad you like them,' answered Jane. 'I wasn't sure whether you would or not. The bouquet turned out to be bigger than I expected.'

'Hold the line a minute, will you?' Stan asked, and Jane heard him say, 'Beat it, Mitzi, will you? Can't a fellow have a little privacy once in a while in his own home?' Then he continued, 'I just wish I'd been awake when you came over. I told Mom she should have called me. I'm sure sorry I couldn't phone you last Saturday.'

'That's all right,' said Jane and then added guardedly,

because her mother was in the next room, 'I thought you might be mad at me because of what happened that morning. You know. In front of Julie's house.'

'I guess I was sort of mad at first.' Stan's voice was also guarded, and Jane knew that his mother and Mitzi were near. 'But that was just because – well, because I wished it was me instead of Buzz.'

'Oh.' It was all Jane could say, and even though she was alone in the hall she could feel herself blush with pleasure.

'Would you mind?' Stan's voice was almost a whisper.

'No.' Jane could barely whisper back, she felt so stifled by emotion.

Then Stan spoke in a normal voice. 'I'll be back at school in time for the steak bake and movie at Woodmont Park. Is it a date?'

'Yes, it is,' answered Jane. 'I'm glad you'll be well in time.'

'I'll call you before then,' promised Stan. 'I'll call you often.'

When Stan had hung up, Jane sat motionless, smiling dreamily at the telephone. Stan wanted to kiss her! She glanced at the calendar that hung above the telephone and saw that the steak bake was two weeks away. Two long weeks! How could she live that long?

CHAPTER

11

THE next two weeks passed quickly for Jane. It did not take long for the story of her walk behind the screen of gladiolas and delphiniums to spread through Woodmont High. Everyone laughed at the story, but the laughter was friendly. *And all because I kept my head up during the whole awful thing,* Jane thought, *and if I had walked down the street cringing with embarrassment, everyone would be making fun of me now.* Instead, boys she did not know, even seniors, grinned at her as they passed her in the corridor and called out, 'Hi there! Picked any petunias lately?' or 'How are things in Birnam wood?' Girls said, 'How did you *ever* do it? Didn't you just about *die* of embarrassment?' The gossip column of the *Woodmontonian* printed an item that asked, 'What sophomore was seen hiding behind a floral duck blind on her way to visit what junior at Cronk Memorial Hospital?' Even the faculty must have heard the story, because the football coach and the physics teacher smiled at Jane as she walked down the hall.

Best of all, Stan telephoned every day at four o'clock, and Jane spent a happy hour on the telephone saying nothing in particular, just talking to Stan. She longed for the day when she could see him again, free from the listening ears of her mother and his little sister. She turned over in her mind what Stan had said about wishing he had been the one to kiss her, not Buzz, and she wondered if he would remember on the night of the steak bake. Perhaps he would ask her to walk under the trees along the stream. . . .

It seemed no time at all until that evening arrived and Jane was actually alone with Stan, riding toward Woodmont Park with him in his blue car. He was even better-looking than she had remembered. His profile was clean-cut and his skin a scrubbed golden tan. The evening was warm, and he was wearing a white shirt with the sleeves rolled up, revealing his identification bracelet on his strong right wrist – a bracelet that he might some day ask her to wear. Jane glanced down at his shoes. Even by the dim light of the dashboard she could see that they had been polished until they gleamed. Jane smiled secretly to herself and felt some of her old shyness return. She had been at ease talking to Stan over the telephone, but now that she was beside him she could think of nothing to say.

Stan took his eyes off the road long enough to glance down at Jane. 'This beats walking, doesn't it?' he remarked. 'Or riding in the Doggie Diner truck.'

Jane laughed. 'It certainly does.'

'You know something?' said Stan. 'The first time I took you out, Dad said I had to be in by ten-thirty. He wouldn't let me take the car, either. I was worried about how I was going to take you to the movies and get you home and still get home myself. I knew Dad wouldn't care if I came in five or ten minutes late, but it was cutting things pretty close. So I took a chance and rode over to your house on my bike. I rode past on the other side of the street first to see if anyone was looking, and when I didn't see anyone I hid my bike in your shrubbery. I was sure scared somebody would look out the window and see me. I didn't want you to think I was just a kid who rode around on a bike.'

Jane smiled to herself before she answered demurely, 'I knew about the bike. After I turned out the light that evening I saw you pull it out of the shrubbery and ride it down the street.'

'You did!' Stan was astonished. 'You knew and you never mentioned it?'

'I didn't say anything, because I knew if you hid your bicycle in the shrubbery you didn't want me to know about it,' Jane explained. 'I was glad you rode it over to my house, because then I was pretty sure you weren't too grown-up to like me. You seemed so much older at first.'

'Well, for Pete's sake!' Stan laughed. 'And here I was feeling so awkward and thought you had so much poise!'

'You know,' said Jane thoughtfully, when they had finished laughing, 'it's funny about bicycles. I never ride mine any more. For some reason, when you're in high school it won't do to be seen riding a bicycle because you need it to get someplace, but it's all right to ride one for fun if you don't really need to. Like going on a picnic or something.'

'That's right,' agreed Stan. 'That's exactly how it is.' They smiled at each other, pleased to have shared this understanding. Jane was sorry they were going to the steak bake. It was so wonderful to be with Stan once more. She wanted to ride on and on through the warm fall evening.

Stan parked his car at the edge of Woodmont Park and

went around to help Jane out. A noisy crowd was gathered under the lights around the barbecue pits, and the smell of cooking steak mingled with the fragrance of the bay and redwood trees. 'I'm starved,' said Stan. 'Come on, let's join the others.'

'Hello, Jane.' 'Hi, Stan, glad to see you back.' 'Hi there, Jane.' 'Stan, you're looking swell.' The crowd welcomed them.

'Hi, everybody,' said Stan, while Jane smiled happily beside him. Not many sophomores had dates for the junior-class steak bake.

Mr Degenkalb, a history teacher who was the harried class adviser, was herding the crowd into line beside the barbecue pits where the steaks were sizzling on grates over open fires. Greg and another boy were turning the steaks with pitchforks. Jane and Stan took their place in line and picked up knives and forks and paper plates. Someone served them scalloped potatoes that had been cooked in the school cafeteria and rushed to the park; someone else put steak on their plates.

'Hi, you two,' said Buzz, who was serving salad. 'I'm on garbage detail.'

'Looks to me like you're serving salad,' remarked Stan, as Jane held out her plate.

'You know how salad turns into garbage when it's been sitting around a couple of hours,' said Buzz. 'That's why I'm on garbage detail.' He ladled some limp greens on to Stan's plate. 'Have some tossed green salad. Take it and toss it into the rubbish bin.'

'Buzz, you're awful,' laughed Jane.

'Come on, Jane,' whispered Stan. 'Let's not sit at the tables with the others. Let's go over by the stream.'

Jane's smile was her answer. Now she knew that Stan wanted to be alone with her as much as she wanted to be alone with him. Carrying their paper plates of food, they walked through the carpet of wood sorrel that grew along the bank of the stream and found two rocks near the trickle of water. It was a perfect spot to be with Stan. There was even a full moon rising through the bay trees. Jane sat down on her rock with a sigh of pleasure. It was a beautiful, romantic moonlit night. Perhaps after Stan had eaten his steak he would turn to her and look deep into her eyes. . . .

'This stream doesn't have much water in it, but at least it's wet,' observed Stan, settling himself on his rock.

'It's the only stream I know of around here that has any water at all this time of the year,' said Jane, as she eyed her steak. It was large and thin and overhung the edges of the paper plate. It did not look like any cut of meat her mother had ever ordered from Jakc's Market. Jane set her plate on her knees and took a bite of cold scalloped potato. Perhaps if she ate her potatoes first there would be more room for the steak on her plate. She sampled the salad. Buzz was right.

Here goes, thought Jane, and sawed at her steak with her cafeteria knife. Nothing happened to the steak, but the pressure of the knife bent the paper plate. Gingerly she tried another side of the steak. This time she succeeded in separating a morsel of meat, which she put into her mouth. That was her mistake. She chewed and chewed and chewed. From the tables by the barbecue pits she could hear laughter and chatter from the crowd, snatches of song, cries of 'Speech!' She was missing the fun, but she didn't care. She was alone with Stan. Alone and chewing.

Stan, too, was occupied with chewing. He gulped, and turned to Jane. 'It sure is a beautiful night, isn't it?' he asked softly, and looked into her eyes.

Jane stopped chewing. She hadn't expected this from Stan so soon, before he had finished his steak.

'Isn't it, Jane?' he asked, as if her answer were important to him.

Jane gulped and swallowed her meat whole. 'Yes, it is,' she said nervously. The moment was so terribly important. 'It's – it's a good cat-fight night.'

Stan looked so startled that Jane immediately regretted the words that had slipped out. 'I mean that's something we always say at home when there's a full moon,' she said, and wished she hadn't. Now she had to go on and explain why the Purdys said a moonlit night was a good cat-fight night. 'When Sir Puss was younger he always got into fights when there was a full moon. Now he goes out and hunts mostly. You know how it is. A good cat-fight night is a sort of family phrase.' *Oh*, she thought, why do I have to babble on this way? Stan was looking into my eyes and now I've spoiled everything.

'Sure, I know,' said Stan, applying his knife to his steak. 'At our house we always call a clear windy day a good drying day. Where we lived in the city there was so much fog Mom always had a hard time getting the washing dry, and almost every morning she would look out the window and say hopefully, "Maybe today will be a good drying day."'

I guess that ought to take care of the weather for a while, thought Jane, and attacked her steak once more. As she sawed away, she glanced at Stan to see how he was managing and found him watching to see how she was cutting her meat. All at once the humour of the situation struck Jane and she began to giggle.

Stan relaxed and laughed. 'Why don't we just pick it up and gnaw?' he suggested.

'I don't know how else we can manage,' agreed Jane, and took her cold steak in both hands. She was careful to tear off a small bite in case Stan should look into her eyes again. Resolutely she and Stan chewed.

'At least tonight we know we're eating meat,' said Jane. 'That night we had dinner in Chinatown I didn't know what anything was. We had just walked past one of those herb shops that has all those weird-looking things in the window and a grocery store that had a tub full of snails, and my imagination went to work. And I wanted to be so sophisticated, too.'

Stan laughed. 'I knew you weren't having a good time, but I didn't know it was that bad.'

Jane chewed thoughtfully. She really had changed since that night in Chinatown. Tonight, only a month instead of ten years later, she could look back on that dinner at Hing Sun Yee's and not only laugh, but admit to Stan she had tried to be sophisticated. And the first time she had a date with Stan she had been so nervous she could scarcely eat a dish of vanilla ice-cream, and now look at her. Here she was, sitting on a rock holding a tough piece of meat in her hands and gnawing at it – and laughing about it.

'Look at the lovebirds over there by the stream,' Jane heard someone on the nearby path say. She winced, and hoped Stan had not heard. He appeared to be concentrating on chewing. Jane considered the size of her meat and the time it took to chew each bite. At this rate, if they were going to finish their steaks they would have to take them along to the movie.

'I give up,' said Stan at last, setting his plate on a rock and wiping his hands on his paper napkin. 'This is too tough for human consumption. It's tougher than Doggie Diner meat.'

'It certainly is,' agreed Jane, as she searched for her paper napkin. She could not find it, so she set her plate aside and surreptitiously wiped her fingers on the edge of her slip. When she looked at Stan he was rubbing one finger back and forth over the name plate on his identification bracelet.

'Jane . . .' Stan looked into her eyes.

Jane felt her heart begin to pound. Nervously she moistened her lips.

'*There* you are!' shouted a voice behind them. It was Buzz, with Julie beside him. 'What are you trying to do? Hide? We've looked all over for you.'

'Hi,' said Stan, with no enthusiasm at all.

Jane flashed her best friend a Julie-how-could-you-look, which Julie returned with an I-know-but-what-could-I-do expression.

Buzz sprang on to a rock and with a sweeping gesture of his right hand proclaimed, 'What is this atomic age we live in? May we by simply touching a button or turning a knob –'

'This isn't your public-speaking class,' interrupted Stan.

'No, but it's a good place to practise,' said Buzz, in his ordinary voice, before he continued eloquently, 'How can we prepare ourselves for what lies ahead?'

'Come on, Buzz,' said Julie. 'We can prepare ourselves for the movie by finding seats.'

Buzz ignored her. 'Today's generation can be the salvation of tomorrow,' he announced, with a sweep of his hand.

Darn Buzz, anyway, thought Jane. He's doing this on purpose, because he knows Stan and I want to be alone.

Stan glowered at Buzz. 'Come on Jane, let's find a rubbish bin for the remains.'

' "Four score and seven years ago –" ' said Buzz. 'What's the matter, Stan? Don't you like my public speaking?'

'No, I don't,' said Stan.

'I'm cut to the quick,' said Buzz cheerfully. 'Mr Chairman, members of the faculty, and fellow students, I stand here before you today to ask you to consider the merits of adopting a twelve-month school year for Woodmont High School.'

Jane gave Julie a do-something-quick look.

Julie flashed Jane an I'll-do-the-best-I-can look. 'Come on, Buzz,' she said. 'The movie is about to start. Let's go and find good seats before they're all taken.'

'Let it start,' said Buzz. 'I found out what it's going to be.'

'What?' Julie asked.

'*The John Quincy Adams Story*,' said Buzz.

Julie groaned. 'Not really! Why did they have to go and choose something like that?'

'Probably because it is pure, high-minded, and educational,' answered Buzz.

'Come on, Jane,' whispered Stan. 'Let's ditch the movie and go for a ride.'

'O.K.' Jane's answer was eager. She could not bear the thought of sitting through a movie, any movie, on such a beautiful night. Not when she could be riding under the stars with Stan.

'Good idea, Stan,' said Buzz heartily. 'Julie and I have been wondering when you were going to ask us to go for a ride in that rumble seat.'

'I didn't,' said Stan flatly. 'Come on, Jane. Let's go.'

Jane clambered up the bank beside Stan and dropped her paper plate into a rubbish bin. Buzz and Julie followed close behind, and Jane hoped that she and Stan would be able to shake them. The junior class, unaware that it was about to see *The John Quincy Adams Story*, was assembling on the benches in front of a motion-picture screen.

Mr Degenkalb, still looking harried, was rounding up the stray members of the class. 'Well, Stan, you're not trying to run out on us, are you?' he asked jovially.

'Well, uh —' said Stan.

'Come on, there are plenty of good seats left,' said Mr Degenkalb, and herded Jane and Stan toward the benches. Out of the corner of her eye Jane noticed Buzz seize Julie by the arm and hurry her out of the park. From the sidewalk he grinned, and waved at Jane and Stan. That Buzz! thought Jane bitterly.

'Let's sit in the last row,' whispered Stan. 'Then we can slip out as soon as they turn off the park lights and the movie starts.' They found seats on the end of a bench in the very last row, back under the redwood trees, and sat down, confident that they could get away soon. One by one, the park lights blinked out and Jane sat poised on the edge of the bench ready to flee with Stan to the privacy of his car.

'Say, Stan,' whispered Mr Degenkalb, 'would you mind moving over?'

Jane and Stan exchanged one stricken look. Silently they moved over, and Mr Degenkalb sat down beside Stan. Jane leaned back on the bench. There was no chance of getting away now. They were trapped. Trapped for all six or eight or maybe even ten reels of *The John Quincy Adams Story*. I can't stand it, thought Jane. I simply cannot stand it. An entire evening wasted, an evening that she wanted to spend riding through the moonlight with Stan, the evening she had waited for so long. For days she had dreamed of this date. ... Well, here they were. Trapped with Mr Degenkalb and John Quincy Adams.

The title of the movie flashed on the screen and the junior class groaned. John Quincy Adams, secretary of state, and John Quincy Adams, sixth president of the United States, moved before Jane's eyes, but all she noticed were the magnified shadows of moths that flew between the projection machine and the screen. The junior class applauded wildly for the moths. The bench grew harder by the minute. Even the rocks by the stream had seemed softer. Two by two, the members of the junior class slipped off the benches and, crouching low beneath the light of the projector, fled from the park.

Jane looked wistfully after these students, these fortunate escapees, who were dispersing to Nibley's or the Woodmont Cinema, where a good movie was playing, or to their cars, and thought longingly of the front seat of Stan's car. If they could only get away they could drive up in the hills, where the night would be aromatic with the scent of eucalyptus trees. She would feel the wind in her hair and when they came to Lookout Point ...

Jane stole a glance at Stan. He was looking straight

ahead and his expression was serious, as if he were absorbed in the activities of John Quincy Adams as secretary of state.

And when they came to Lookout Point, Jane's thought ran on, Stan would park the car so it faced the view of the bay and the city, and he would turn off the ignition and turn to her in the moonlight and say ...

There was no use thinking about it, Jane told herself. Not when they were practically surrounded by Mr Degenkalb. But she did not know what else she could think about. Certainly not John Quincy Adams, not on a night like this. Everything had looked so hopeful when she and Stan were sitting on the rocks by the stream, but life never turned out the way she planned. Oh well, there would be other dates of course, but it would have been so nice if ...

Jane felt Stan's hand brush hers, but when she looked up at him in the flickering light he was staring straight ahead. She was surprised to feel his hand on her arm and still more surprised – almost unbelieving – to see his fingers unclasp his identification bracelet and remove it from his arm. Silently he fumbled with the bracelet and slipped it around her right wrist. With a tiny click he snapped the clasp shut. Jane gave a gasp of astonishment and turned questioningly to Stan. She was wearing his identification bracelet! The silver links on her wrist were still warm from his arm.

Stan leaned toward Jane. 'O.K.?' he whispered.

'Yes,' she whispered back and smiled radiantly at Stan, at John Quincy Adams, at the backs of the rapidly diminishing junior class. She really was wearing Stan's bracelet on her arm, something she had scarcely allowed herself to think about – at least not often; it would be so far in the future, if it happened at all. And now it had happened, months before she had dreamed it could. Jane's wrist felt small and feminine in the circle of heavy silver links. Tenderly she caressed the letters of Stan's name with her finger tips. Stanley Crandall. The nicest boy in the whole world.

After that it seemed only a few minutes until the movie ended and the lights in the park went on. 'Well, Stan,' said Mr Degenkalb, 'it was a pretty good movie, wasn't it?'

Dreamily Jane wondered how Stan would answer. He laughed easily and said, 'Especially the parts played by moths.' Then he took Jane by the hand – something he had never done before. 'Come on, let's get out of here,' he said, and pulled her through the crowd to his car.

Finally after hours – no, days – of waiting, Jane was alone with Stan. She climbed up into the seat and looked at her watch by moonlight. 'Stan,' she wailed, when she saw the time. 'It's twenty-five minutes past ten. I have to go home.' Only five minutes left to be with Stan. This was the way things always turned out for her.

Stan started the car and headed toward Blossom Street. 'Jane,' he said urgently, above the sound of the model-A motor, 'you know what it means to wear a fellow's bracelet?'

'Yes,' answered Jane breathlessly.

'It means you're going steady.'

'I know.' Jane touched the bracelet.

'You really want to?'

'Yes, Stan. I really want to.'

Stan stopped the car in front of Jane's house. 'I wish it wasn't so late,' he said, and ran around the car to open the door for her. He took her hand in his as they went up the walk together. Half-way to the house Stan stopped and turned to Jane. He put his hands on her shoulders and drew her toward him. 'I'm glad we're going steady,' he whispered.

'So am I.' In spite of the reassuring weight of his bracelet on her wrist, Jane suddenly felt shy. It seemed strange to be so close to Stan, to feel his crisp clean shirt against her cheek. She could not look up at him. Gently Stan lifted her face to his. 'You're my girl,' he whispered.

At that moment they both heard the strange, muted cry of a cat that has successfully stalked and killed. Jane stiffened. Sir Puss appeared from the shrubbery and tossed his catch into the air so that it landed with a thud at Jane's feet. Crying insistently, the cat hovered over his prey. He would, she knew, cry until he was praised.

Jane felt Stan start to pull away from her. Then he hesitated and quickly bent his face to hers. Their noses bumped, but their lips met tenderly, clumsily, one side of his mouth against one side of hers. Jane had not known a boy's lips could be so soft. Stan's first kiss – it was a moment to cherish.

Persistently Sir Puss cried over his trophy. A window flew open, and Jane stepped away from Stan. The beam of a flashlight played over the yard and settled on the cat and his catch. 'My, that's a big one!' said Mr Purdy, still half asleep. The cat, satisfied that his good work had been recognized, silently picked up his gopher and disappeared into the bushes. 'Why, hello there, Jane.' Mr Purdy sounded bewildered. 'You home already?'

'Yes, Pop,' answered Jane. First the cat, now her father! 'Well, I guess I'd better be going,' said Stan awkwardly.

'Good night, Stan,' said Jane softly. 'I had a wonderful time.'

Stan started down the walk toward his car. 'Good night, Stan,' called Mr Purdy.

'Good night, sir,' Stan called back. 'I'll see you to-morrow Jane.'

Smiling to herself, Jane turned and walked toward the house. She was Stan's girl. That was all that really mattered.